THE HOUSE OF
SEVEN MABELS

THE HOUSE OF SEVEN MABELS

A Jane Jeffry Mystery

JILL CHURCHILL

WILLIAM MORROW
An Imprint of HarperCollins*Publishers*

HarperCollins books may be purchased for educational, business, or sales promotional use. For information please write: Special Markets Department, HarperCollins Publishers Inc., 10 East 53rd Street, New York, NY 10022.

FIRST EDITION

Printed on acid-free paper

Designed by Sarah Maya Gubkin

Library of Congress Cataloging-in-Publication Data

Churchill, Jill, 1943–
    The house of seven Mabels : a Jane Jeffry mystery / Jill Churchill.
—1st ed.
        p. cm.
    ISBN 0-380-97736-2
    1. Jeffry, Jane (Fictitious character)—Fiction. 2. Women detectives—Illinois—Chicago—Fiction. 3. Dwellings—Remodeling—Fiction. 4. Single mothers—Fiction. 5. Suburban life—Fiction. 6. Chicago (Ill.)—Fiction. I. Title.

PS3553.H85 H68   2002
813'.54—dc21

                                                        2001044985

02   03   04   05   06   WB/RRD   10   9   8   7   6   5   4   3   2   1

THE HOUSE OF
SEVEN MABELS

1

Jane Jeffry had seen her son Mike off to his second year of college several weeks ago. Her daughter, Katie, started her senior year in high school, and younger son Todd moved to ninth grade. This time next year, she'd have only one child to take care of on a daily basis. And Todd would be at the age when no young man wants to hang out with his mother. He already was.

She was sitting at her kitchen table, idly flipping through her calendar. It used to be full of notations, but except for a dentist appointment in three weeks and a hair salon appointment to touch up her roots, the pages were nearly blank.

As Jane was pondering this wistfully, her next-door neighbor and best friend, Shelley Nowack, turned into her own driveway, which adjoined Jane's. Not quite fast enough to touch the pavement on only two wheels, but giving that impression. The tires of her minivan squealed as she slammed on the brakes. This was her normal mode of driving.

Shelley tapped on the kitchen door just as Jane was opening it. "You look glum," Shelley said. "I have something to cheer you up. Remember that old Victorian house that turned into such a blight when some fool divided it into crummy apartments and the druggies took it over?"

"Who wouldn't? It was one of our larger civic battles, getting the lowdown on the zoning. Someone was supposed to tear it down, I thought. Why's it still standing?"

"Because Bitsy bought it to restore."

"Bitsy?"

"You don't remember Bitsy?" Shelley asked.

"I do remember her, if you mean Bitsy Burnside. The all-time Queen of Room Mothers. I never knew a woman who could turn something like that into a full-time job."

"Bitsy's past that stage," Shelley said, airily waving this recollection aside. "Her kids are grown. She divorced that overbearing stockbroker husband and must have taken him to the cleaners. And there's gossip that she also got a huge inheritance from a childless oil baron great-uncle."

"Wow. No wonder Bitsy's moving into real estate. Why don't things like that happen to us?"

"Luck of the draw, I suppose," Shelley said.

"But even if she has wads of money, what the devil does she know about renovating a wreck of a house?"

Shelley shrugged. "I suppose with enough cash, you can buy very good advice."

"I guess I wish her well."

"Perk up, Jane. She wants to talk to us over lunch tomorrow."

"Why? She's a dangerous person to talk to. Every time I let her bend my ear, I ended up making two hundred strings of paper garlands or baking fifty-five highly decorated cupcakes."

"Because she wants to hire us."

"To make garlands?"

"Jane, get a grip and forget about garlands. And quit lolling about with your elbows on the table and make us a big pot of coffee. Use the good kind. Bitsy wants us to be her decorators. A paying job that requires a lot of shopping."

Jane's eyes lit up for a moment. "Paid to go shopping? Who would have thought life had such a thing in store for us, so to speak? But what do we know about decorating that everyone else doesn't know more about?"

"I guess she thinks we have good taste," Shelley said.

"She thinks we're patsies," Jane said, turning the tables on Shelley, who was usually the more cynical one. "I tell you, Shelley, this is going to involve something we really don't want to do. She'd be doing it herself if it were a desirable thing for her to spend time on."

"You really are grouchy today, aren't you?"

"I'm bored," Jane admitted. "I'm so seldom bored that it makes me cranky."

Widowed when her husband died in a car accident years earlier, Jane thought she'd done a pretty good job raising her children. Mike and Todd were normal boys, interested in girls and cars, but not doing anything remarkably stupid about either.

That she knew of.

Katie was a normal teenage girl, which is to say a bundle of conflicting personalities, and extremely high maintenance. Katie, who had recently decided she wanted to be called Katherine, sometimes regarded her mother as her archenemy, always as the source of food, money, and housing, and more and more frequently, as a semi-friend.

But who am I? Jane had been wondering lately. Her role as daily cook, car pool driver, arbitrator of sibling rivalry outbreaks, and soother of hurt feelings was nearly over.

"Then this is the perfect time to turn your time and attention to something new and different," Shelley said with remarkably good cheer. "Make us that coffee before I need intravenous caffeine."

Jane got up and filled the coffeemaker, saying as she did so, "I see your point. Really I do. Our attempts to be wedding planners went up in flames. But we both need something to do now that we're free of little children. The only thing we're really good at is shopping. But I don't think this is it."

What Jane really meant was that Shelley loved shopping for anything. Jane wasn't half as enthusiastic, but had recently sprung for a few luxuries and enjoyed spending a little money on herself for a change.

"It won't hurt to let Bitsy pay for a very nice lunch before we decide that," Shelley said, drumming a perfectly manicured nail impatiently on the kitchen table.

"I guess not," Jane said. "Decorators? Hmm."

". . . and this lunch is at Michelle's Bistro."

"Oh?"

"Did I forget to tell you about it?" Shelley asked. "A cousin of mine hosted a family party there a month ago, with all our aunts and the other woman cousins, and it's divine. Tall food."

"Tall food?" Jane said, watching for the instant the coffee could be served so Shelley would stop that irritating tapping on the table with her fingernails.

"You know, that trendy stuff with an artful blob of sauce, a piece of fish or meat, and stuff piled on top of it in towers."

"Yeah, the kind of place you have to put on pantyhose and jewelry for," Jane said with a smile. "For a good free meal, I'll listen nicely to anyone who has anything to say. And come home and think about it while I digest the food."

When the coffee was ready and Jane and Shelley

had both knocked back a bit of it and sighed with satisfaction, Shelley said, "Now, Jane, there's something else you need to know about this."

"Ah-hah! The Big Drawback! I knew there was one."

"I'm not sure it is, but here's the deal. Bitsy's fallen in with a somewhat rabid group of feminists. Suddenly she's single, her kids are grown, she's wallowing in money, and she starts a new life."

"No more cupcakes, huh?"

Shelley ignored this comment. "So this renovation is sort of part of that."

"What does that mean? 'Sort of?' " Jane asked.

Shelley brushed back an errant bit of her bangs—nervously, Jane thought, because Shelley's dark cap of hair was always neat and tidy.

"It's this way. She's chosen a female contractor and mostly hiring women workers."

Jane looked at Shelley for a long moment, then said, "How'd she find these people? When was the last time you had a girly-girly plumber fix your drains?"

"Now, Jane, don't go sexist on me," Shelley objected. "What is there to plumbing that a woman couldn't do if she wanted or needed to?"

"That's just it, Shelley. I never had the urge to investigate being a plumber even though I wield a mean plunger when I'm forced to. The difference between needing to become your own plumber at times and the desire to do it as a full-time job isn't a concept I grasp. Yes, I've dealt with stuffed toys going down the drains, but when the sewer backs up in the basement during a flood, I call a man to fix it. Men don't have much of a sense of smell. And I write the check."

"And it's a substantial check, Jane. Why shouldn't an able-bodied woman get the money?"

"I don't object to that happening," Jane said. "I've just never heard of a woman plumber."

"But Bitsy and her contractor have," Shelley said.

"Okay, okay. For a really good lunch at someone else's expense, I'll go and listen to what she has to say. But I'll have to borrow a pair of pantyhose. I ran my last ones while I was replacing the upstairs bathroom toilet seal ring," Jane joked.

"Sure you did," Shelley said with a grin. "The only reason you know that a toilet *has* a seal ring is because you're hung up on that do-it-yourself channel. I've caught you watching it three times now. I know you're secretly interested in this."

"Secretly, maybe. Reluctantly, for sure."

2

Michelle's Bistro looked like a classy place to Jane. Shelley's highly successful businessman husband, who entertained a lot, probably wouldn't have been as impressed. It was one of the few stand-alone buildings in a new upscale mall. It looked like something that should have been perched above the Mediterranean Sea in southern France, clinging to rock face instead of what had recently been flat Illinois farmland.

Jane had dressed to the nines, found a pair of pantyhose without runs, even gone to the hairdresser earlier in the day to get her roots touched up. A hostess all in black greeted them and showed them to a secluded table at the west end of the surprisingly large restaurant. As they made their way across, Jane noticed that there were virtually no men in sight. There were only a couple of somewhat frightened-looking husbands and a busboy who looked androgynous enough to qualify as a girl.

"Is this where the well-bred feminists eat?" Jane whispered to Shelley, who stopped dead and looked around.

Shelley looked genuinely surprised. "I didn't notice that there were so few men when I was here before. I guess they can't legally disallow them."

Jane made a muffled groaning sound, and they plowed along in the wake of the hostess, who had a long, fierce stride.

Two women were already seated at the table. Bitsy Burnside was almost unrecognizable. She'd cropped her hair short and must have had a great deal of plastic surgery since Jane had last seen her. Her eyes used to crinkle in a really cute way when she smiled. Now there was no sign of a line on her face as she rose, smiling, to greet them.

"I'm so glad you came. I can't wait to tell you all about my project." It was a banquette table, and Bitsy gestured for Jane and Shelley to sit in the middle between her and the other woman.

We're being trapped, Jane thought.

"This is Ms. Sandra Anderson," Bitsy said when the other woman also stepped out to shake hands. "Formerly Mrs. Somebody." Bitsy and her companion both laughed at this. "She took her mother's maiden name as her own when she divorced him. She's my contractor."

Jane considered this matrilineal introduction and wished she had the nerve to mention that the woman's mother's maiden name had almost certainly been her father's name all along. But this wasn't the time to pick a fight. Maybe after lunch had been paid for.

Sandra Anderson, or Sandy, as Bitsy called her, was a very tall woman wearing a knockoff Armani suit in gray and taupe. The way the sleeve cuff wrinkled slightly was a tipoff that it wasn't the real thing, Jane assumed. Sandra, like Bitsy, had hair styled as a man would, but her face hadn't been done. She looked tough as nails, with a corrugated forehead and long, sad lines around her lips.

Jane scooted in and was next to Sandra, who carried a fairly large purse with a strap over her opposite shoulder. Shelley had left a space between herself and Jane to put their purses.

"Want to pile that purse up with ours?" Jane asked Sandra.

Sandra looked shocked. "No, thank you," she said, as if the suggestion had been inappropriate.

"Let's order before we get to business," Bitsy said. "I've already asked for a bottle of the house merlot. You'll love it."

A silence fell and Jane filled it. "Bitsy, I've always wondered what your real name is."

"I'm afraid it's really Bitsy. My parents were from Savannah and Southerners often do awful things like this to baby girls," Bitsy said. It was obviously a well-rehearsed line she'd developed over the years of being asked this question. "It was part of Itsy Bitsy Baby, of course, and thank heaven they didn't give me that whole name. I had an awful time getting a passport until I showed them my birth certificate that clearly stated that Bitsy is my real name."

Everybody laughed sympathetically, then fell on their menus for lack of a suitable subject for more chitchat.

"Jane, you must try the filet mignon," Shelley said. "I had that the first time I was here and it was so good I'm having it again."

Jane noticed it was the priciest of the entrees. Shelley was really going out of her way to make sure Jane got her money's worth out of this meal.

The waitress, also dressed all in black, brought their drinks and recommended the filet as their house specialty, along with the vegetarian version, which made Jane's skin crawl to consider. Bitsy and Sandy ordered meatless salads, and Jane and Shelley ordered the real filet.

Bitsy immediately launched into her spiel. "I've had extraordinarily good luck to be able to afford to get into this renovation. I thought I should let you know what my intentions are. Many corporations have their headquarters in Chicago. Often they bring in their suppliers or people they want to hire and wish to impress. Shelley's husband is a good example."

Shelley looked at her blankly, wondering just what Bitsy thought she knew about Paul. He had been born poor and Polish and had built up a chain of cheap Greek fast-food restaurants. He'd clawed his way up from a run-down two-bedroom house he'd shared with his parents and seven siblings, and when he and Shelley entertained Paul's friends, employees, suppliers, and neighbors, it was for the pure pleasure of doing so. A pleasure for him, at least. Not always for Shelley.

"The house I've selected is very close to the El line," Bitsy plowed on, "so it's handy to the city. Although I suspect most of the people who will be using the home will be chauffeured to the city anyway. I intend to provide—for a hefty fee—one or more of these corporations with the perfect home to house their most important guests when they visit."

"Sounds like a good idea," Jane admitted.

"So it has to be the height of luxury," Bitsy said, preening. "A main kitchen always stocked with elegant foods and suitable for catering. Bathrooms to die for. The best and biggest beds and the best real linens. Complete privacy between the two wings, which will both have access to the kitchen. That way two groups can stay there without running into one another. Well-stocked bars in the suites. Banquet facilities. Elegant furnishings . . ."

"Is that where we come in?" Jane asked.

"Exactly!" Bitsy exclaimed. "I've been in Shelley's home and it's lovely. I assume that since you live next door and are good friends, yours is lovely as well."

Jane just smiled at Bitsy's misapprehension of Jane's decorating skills. Shelley made a noise that could have been a sneeze, or more likely a subdued snort.

"I have the paperwork to let you into the professional decorators' place downtown," Bitsy said proudly.

"The Merchandise Mart?" Shelley asked, impressed.

"What we want is sheer elegance, with a slight hint of Victoriana. Suitable to an old Victorian house, you see. But not feminine. There probably won't be very many wives coming along, but every detail must suit them when they do accompany a husband."

This seemed odd to Jane. Such ardent feminists speaking of women merely as wives. "What about that woman who is the president and CEO of eBay?" she asked.

"What's eBay?" Sandra asked.

Shelley nudged Jane. Jane didn't understand the nudge unless it meant, "Keep your trap shut," which it probably did.

"Never mind," Shelley said. "I think we understand."

The food arrived and they abandoned business talk temporarily. The filets were indeed the best Jane had tasted. Tiny but thick. Perfectly cooked. They sat in solitary splendor in a pool of divinely rich brown gravy, piled high with chunks of an unfamiliar but good cheese, with frilly baby celery stalks impaled on the cheese. *Anything for height,* Jane thought to herself. There were barely cooked tiny peas to the side with shreds of mint scattered on them, and a log of scalloped potatoes, adorned with finely minced basil.

The other two women's salads likewise were works of art. Exotic greens and tiny fruits Jane couldn't identify, along with lightly cooked pearl onions, baby yellow-skinned potatoes, more frilly celery, and julienned peppers in red, green, purple, and yellow.

Even if she and Shelley turned down the job they were being offered, this was truly a meal she'd never forget.

A meal to die for, she thought, not meaning to be prophetic.

3

Jane had to undo a button on the waistband of her knockout green silk suit on the way home. Shelley had forced her to buy it on sale a couple of months earlier.

"I'm a blimp," Jane said. "I should have worn something larger to eat so much. That raspberry chocolate torte put me over the brink."

"I told you you'd get a good meal out of the meeting," Shelley said smugly.

"Are you really thinking of doing this?" Jane said, trying not to see how fast the landscape was zipping by. She was afraid to lean over and see what speed Shelley was going.

"I think it's something we should at least consider," Shelley said. "We're to see the house tomorrow, and

Bitsy says she'll have a contract for us to look over. But frankly, I'm a bit uneasy about it."

"Elaborate, please," Jane said. So far she'd thought she was the only one who didn't wholeheartedly like the prospect.

"For one thing, I don't think Bitsy has a clue what she's gotten into. Contract or no contract, it could turn into a hassle. We'll have to pay a very good lawyer to crawl over it word by word. A couple of hundred dollars up front, I'd guess."

"And?"

"I had a bad feeling about that Sandy woman. She's a tough old gal. But that doesn't mean she knows what she's doing. To find out, we might have to also pay a private investigator who specializes in construction matters. I have no idea how we'd find one, unless Paul knows someone. It's another expense. Unless we can find out about her through a credit bureau or someplace. I don't like spending money just to accept a job."

Shelley managed to coolly pass a car on the on-ramp, and Jane had to close her eyes and utter a quick prayer to the gods of traffic. She didn't want to be loaded onto an ambulance with her green silk skirt falling off.

While crossing three lanes full of eighteen-wheelers, Shelley said, "But we may fall in love with the house and have lots of good ideas for the decorating. Who can tell?

We don't have to make an instant decision. Big old houses aren't renovated overnight."

"Could you slow down just a tiny bit?" Jane asked.

"Sure. If you want that forty tons of frozen beef behind me to end up my backseat."

Jane had planned get Todd and Katie carryout for dinner so she could go out with Mel that evening, but he had to cancel their date at the last minute. "Just as I was turning in the last of my paperwork, I was told I'd drawn plainclothes duty for a rock concert," he explained. "I must have really irritated someone up the line to be stuck with this. How about tomorrow night? If I survive?"

Jane could afford to be gracious about this. After all, she'd eaten so much at lunch she couldn't have appreciated a real dinner.

So she was stuck at home, all dolled up and nowhere to go. She put her fancy suit away and donned her most disreputable baggy jeans and T-shirt that should have gone in the trash at least six months earlier.

She'd recently given in and put a television and a bookcase in her bedroom. She'd collected all her favorite read-again mysteries from all over the house and put them on the shelves. She settled into bed with Max and Meow on the bedspread and Willard the dog snoring in the corner.

For a while, she watched a bit of her favorite channel, but the thought of a woman building her own two-story deck intimidated her. She flipped to the financial news station briefly, where they were explaining why a stock she held quite a bit of for the kids' college fees had plummeted in value. Flipping the television off, she went to the bookshelf and selected an Agatha Christie book she'd last read so long ago she was sure she wouldn't remember the ending.

That palled when the character she recalled as the murderer appeared on page seven.

She considered taking a nice long, soaky bath, but didn't want to destroy the wonder her hairdresser had created that morning quite yet. She rejected the idea of cruising the kitchen for a snack after consuming such a huge lunch. Nor did taking a brisk walk around the block appeal in spite of the nice early fall evening.

Jane wasn't herself. She prided herself on never being bored. There was always something she'd like to do. Watch an old movie, try out some craft she'd seen demonstrated, or, if at wit's end, get out a big jigsaw puzzle. And somewhat less frequently, work on the novel she'd been plugging away at for years.

Mike was at college, Katie was out at a movie with friends, and Todd was working on his homework in his room. He'd finally decided it might be a hoot to become a good student. This should have cheered her up.

But it didn't, and she realized that she was subconsciously brooding about this job Shelley was so interested in doing. Shelley would be good at it. Shelley's house was as lovely as Bitsy had said. Jane's house was merely a comfortable old place with lots of old family furniture and ornaments she was sentimental about. She had no real confidence in her tastes.

She'd recently had her front hall repapered with something dark she loved at the wallpaper place, but once hung, it made the hall look like a dismal tunnel in one of those video games the kids were so fond of. She half expected a red-eyed monster to leap out of the coat closet.

She had to admit to herself that she'd taken an instant dislike to the Sandra woman. She tried to analyze why that was. It wasn't because the woman wasn't attractive. She had other friends who weren't beauties but had marvelous personalities.

It wasn't even that the woman had never heard of eBay, though she found that peculiar. Jane herself haunted eBay and had found replacements for all the chipped or cracked dishes of her grandmother's set of good china.

Was it the feminist angle that got under her skin? Jane would hate to think that was it. She considered herself a feminist. After all, she'd raised three children by herself after being widowed young, and they were turning out wonderfully. She'd done a good job without a husband. Thanks to having had a financial stake in her late husband's family pharmacy, she'd learned to handle money well. When Mike left for college, she'd had to learn to do a lot of hard work around the house he'd formerly taken care of for her. She'd even gotten a ladder and replaced the stairway light fixture. That was a pretty independent thing to do, even if it scared her to death, perching in midair that way.

That was what feminism meant to her. Being able to take good care of yourself and your children. So why did she feel that a couple of women renovating a house wasn't right? She sensed that Shelley was a bit wary, too. That worried her.

She was no closer to an answer when Katie come home from the movie.

"Vegging out, I see. Your hair looks great. How are you going to keep it that way?" Katie asked, sitting down next to the cats, scritching both their outstretched necks and wiping the fur off her hands onto her mother's bedspread.

"I probably can't, but thanks. I went to the day spa you suggested. You should have warned me, however, how much a cut and color cost. Katie, let me tell you what Shelley and I did today and see what you think."

Jane outlined the scenario. The old Victorian house in such disrepair, what Bitsy and Sandra had said, the odd restaurant full of women and a few frightened men. The plan that she and Shelley would be in charge of the decorating.

"You?" Katie laughed. "What do you know about that?"

"Not a lot, but I could learn by taking this on."

"May I go along?"

Jane was surprised. "Why would you want to?"

Katie shrugged. "My room's been exactly the same all my life."

"Yes. Messy," Jane said.

"I'd love to look at paint chips and cool molding and a neat bed. One of those sleigh things. You know what they are?"

"As it happens, I do," Jane said, half offended.

"So what's the question?" Katie asked.

"I'm reluctant and I can't figure out why," Jane admitted.

"What's Mrs. Nowack think?"

"She likes the idea better than I do, but she has some misgivings, too. To be perfectly honest, I don't think either of us like the people we'd be working for."

Katie grinned. "Remember what you told me when I wanted to change classes because I couldn't stand the way the algebra teacher was always blowing her nose revoltingly?"

"That was different. She was the best algebra teacher in the whole school system. She'd won all sorts of awards."

"Maybe these women you don't like have done that, too."

Jane crawled to the foot of the bed and gave Katie a big hug. "I'm so glad you're growing up so well. Someday you'll be telling me what to do—and God help me, I'll probably listen."

"About time," Katie said, hugging back. "Just make sure you have an escape clause. Give it a shot, Mom. You might enjoy it."

4

The next morning Jane and Shelley put on jeans and old boots and went to look at the house, as Bitsy had instructed them to do at lunch the day before. Shelley had never worn jeans except in her house or her own backyard and was outraged at having to go out in public in them.

Jane, who practically lived in an assortment of faded and well-worn dungarees, as her grandmother had called them, said, "Get over it. We're not going to display you to the public, just a bunch of workers."

Shelley insisted they park behind the big house so no one passing on the street would see her. That was impossible. The backyard, which was enormous and hedged in by old pines, was full of construction materials, Dumpsters with chutes going down to them from windows at the back, and boxes of tools.

They had to back out and park on the street, like everyone else, where Shelley and Jane sat staring at the house. "Look at those gables."

"Shelley, I think a gable is the way to refer to the ends of a house. Those are dormers on the third floor."

"I'd rather think of them as gables. The House of Seven Mabels," she added with a laugh.

Jane liked the term. "It's time we go in, whatever you want to call it."

Shelley practically streaked from the car to the front door. Jane followed more slowly, looking closely at the house. She had driven by it innumerable times, but had only glanced at it disapprovingly. It was really a community eyesore. She was constantly expecting to come by and see it leveled to the ground.

But with a practical reason to study it, she found it interesting.

Everyone called it the old Victorian house, but that was only because of the once fancy trim, Jane decided. Not that Jane knew what made a house Victorian anyway. There was all sorts of elaborate gingerbread siding covering it, but it was only in peeling patches now. Jane could imagine that it had been an eye-stopper when it was new.

She could picture it with stark white paint, lighting up the whole neighborhood. Of course there probably wasn't a neighborhood when it was built. It was the sort of house that had probably stood in solitary splendor alone on a good ten acres.

There was a purely Southern verandah stretched across the front and presumably going around both sides. She hadn't noticed whether it had continued around the back when they attempted to park there. The third floor had a sloping roof and a plethora of dormer windows—which Shelley insisted were called gables.

She approached closer and walked up the four steps to the front of the house. They'd have to replace those steps. She nearly put her foot through one. Maybe narrower steps and a ramp, so it would be accessible to the disabled or wheelchair-bound.

The floor and walls of the verandah, protected from sun and rain for ages, gave a hint of the house's former glory. Jane could have closed her eyes and imagined the seven-foot expanse from the house to the elaborate but broken rails, with floors painted a shiny dark green, pristine white wicker furniture with bright cushions scattered about, and little tables where you could genteelly knock back a couple of frosty glasses of mimosas on a lazy Sunday morning in summer.

If she had the kind of money Bitsy was reputed to have, Jane would happily restore it herself and live there just for the verandah. Think what grand parties you could have on late spring evenings if you planted masses of lilac bushes at the foundation.

Shelley crept back out the front door. "Why are you dawdling out here, Jane?"

"I'm just picturing how it could look. Isn't that what we're supposed to be doing?"

"I guess so," Shelley admitted. "So what do you see doing with this mess?"

Jane described what she had in mind. "In nice weather this could be a divine spot to sit and relax."

"I don't think corporate bigwigs ever relax," Shelley said. "Relaxed bigwigs is an oxymoron."

"They couldn't resist it here," Jane said with assurance.

"We need to start measuring," Shelley said in her bossiest mode. She was fiddling with a notebook with a pencil tied to it with a gold string, and a hefty metal tape measure.

They went through what once had been a spectacular front door, curved at the top, with remnants of deep-purple-blue stained glass arched above it. Carvings of grapes climbing trellises decorated the door itself. But it was in sad shape. Someone had apparently stabbed it at some point. There were deep gashes in the wood, revealing what Jane thought was mahogany.

"We're going to have to learn all about different woods," she said. "Where will we learn that?"

"At the library?" Shelley asked. "There must be tons of books we'll need to consult before we can talk about furniture without making fools of ourselves."

They stepped inside the front door, closing it behind them. Jane closed her eyes for a moment, overwhelmed by memories of some of the old boarding schools in Europe she'd attended as a girl when her parents were traveling all over the world. It was the smell that gripped her. Of course it was overlaid by the odor of garbage and mildew, but under that was the familiar scent of very old wood, beeswax polish, lavender water, camphor oil, and ancient leatherbound books similar to those in some of the old schools she'd attended.

"Jane, are you taking a nap or what?"

"Just smelling the house," Jane said as she opened her eyes, but didn't explain.

The front hall had suffered a great deal of damage as well. It was vast, with a pair of curving staircases ascending upstairs on both sides. They, too, had rails missing, but the treads must have been made of some impervious material, because when Jane tested out walking up a few of them, they felt sturdy. Remnants of striped wallpaper in blue and cream were in tatters. The fancy molding, egg-and-dart pattern (one of the few decorating terms Jane knew) around the room, though coated with dust and grime, seemed to be mostly intact.

"This is going to be the reception area," Bitsy said, appearing from one of the many beat-up doors that opened onto the front hall. "Come along and see the rest of the house."

Bitsy was back to being the perky sort of woman she'd been when she wanted PTA volunteers to ante up money for crepe paper, colored chalk, decorated plastic cups and plates, and far too much of their free time.

They followed her around the ground floor first. Between and behind the pair of curving staircases, they passed through a door to the back half of the house and came out into what must have once been a kitchen, it seemed. Whatever kind of appliances were once there were gone, and dusty wires and stubbed-out pipes gaped out of the walls.

"It's too small, of course," Bitsy said. "I have the chef from Michelle's Bistro coming later in the week to advise us on how much space we need and how to arrange the counters."

"A woman, I assume?" Jane said blandly.

"Of course. There was a pantry off the north side, and what must have been the cook's quarters and a dank little hallway to the basement door. We're taking out the walls and using that space as part of the kitchen. Or we might go the other direction, keeping the pantry and turning the cook's quarters into rest rooms for the staff."

"Hmm," Jane said. "You'd better check codes, Bitsy. I'd guess it's a no-no to have bathrooms open directly off the food-preparation area."

"I hadn't thought of that," Bitsy said. "I wonder why Sandy didn't mention it when we discussed it."

"Maybe because I'm wrong," Jane said with a smile. "What else is on the ground floor?"

Bitsy showed them the back end of the house. What

could have been a sunny breakfast room, or maybe a conservatory, was there. Lots of windows, almost all broken out. There was so much dirt and leaves you could hardly see the surface, but when Jane kicked some away, she uncovered a tile floor, badly cracked. "Are you going to shore this up?" Jane asked as Bitsy and Shelley stepped into the room for a closer look.

"Shore it up?"

"Can't you feel that it's listing away from the house?"

Bitsy took a couple of steps forward. "I see what you mean. Euwww. That means either take it off or do some heavy-duty foundation work. I'll have to think about this. I'd hoped to make it a nice little spot for the staff to take their breaks."

She'd lost her perkiness.

In the center of the south end of the house was a vast dining room that must have been locked off from vandals for decades. It, too, was dusty, and the floral wallpaper was faded. Ancient heavy maroon velvet drapes hung in threadbare tatters at tall windows on the far side. Jane half expected to see Miss Havisham's moldering wedding cake somewhere nearby.

"What have you planned for this area?" Shelley asked.

"I thought I could hire it out for private parties between resident guests. Wedding receptions and such. The French doors behind the curtains used to open to the deck."

Was Bitsy referring to the verandah? Jane wondered. *A deck! Indeed,* Jane thought indignantly.

"But someone tore part of it off," Bitsy went on. "I guess to discourage trespassers and vandals."

"It's certainly better preserved than what we've seen so far," Shelley said.

Bitsy laughed. "Wait until you see the second floor. You'll appreciate this room even more. On the other side of the main hall is a matching space that's going to be all one room for corporate banquets."

She led them through the dining room and into what must have been a generous-size front parlor for guests who merely came to tea. There were more of the floor-to-ceiling doors, glassless now and patched with warped, crumbling plywood.

Jane's imagination ran away with her again. What a nice room this would be as an office. If she were doing this house over for herself, she'd cover the walls with bookshelves. Set up a desk going out into the middle of the room so she could work on her endless novel, or more likely the bill paying, and look out the front windows for inspiration.

She mentally shook herself.

Stop thinking this way, she thought. *You're possibly going to be the hired help, not the mistress of this old mansion.*

5

"Let me take you upstairs now," Bitsy said.

"Wait," Shelley said. "I want to measure every room."

"No need to," Bitsy replied. "Sandy had an architectural engineer out and there are detailed measured plans for each floor, as well as the landscaping. I just need to go pick up a copy for each of you."

"Just the same, I want to measure for myself. It'll make it more meaningful if and when we take on the job," Shelley said in her don't-cross-me voice.

"If and when?" Bitsy asked.

Shelley smiled. "We haven't seen the contract yet."

Bitsy made a half gesture as if to slap her own head. "I had them with me yesterday and completely forgot to give them to you. Come on upstairs and I'll fetch them as you leave. It's a very good contract. You'll agree, I'm sure."

Neither Jane nor Shelley replied to this remark.

She led them up the right-hand curved stairway, which appeared and felt solid all the way up. Jane wondered if this were the single stable element of the house.

When they reached the second floor, it was a total shock. There was only a tiny landing. The other side of the house was blocked off with very old plywood. They turned and looked down a narrow, dirty corridor with rows of dingy doors on both sides and an extraordinarily ugly, brown, worn cheap vinyl flooring on the hall floors.

"I told you you'd be surprised."

"Surprised is hardly the word," Shelley snorted.

"But it's going to be lovely when we finish."

Shelley started walking along the hall, opening doors. The ones that weren't stuck shut revealed tiny rooms, some still with grubby futons on the floors, or ancient bedsteads with disgusting mattresses. The rooms were hardly six feet wide. Trash had been swept into corners, and the floors were bare. Pegs were on all the walls for hanging clothes, instead of providing closets.

"It was for druggies," Bitsy said. "And homeless people, I've been told."

"Someone set it up that way," Jane said. "The people who lived here didn't build these partitions. Who owned this wreck?"

"That's hard to answer and the reason it stood vacant so long," Bitsy said, sounding extremely socially enlightened. "It had belonged to a series of largely fake Middle Eastern holding companies. I'm told there used to be a pair of enormous thugs who came by every week to collect the rents. According to the Realtor who eventually acquired the right to sell it, the thugs didn't even speak English."

"Thugs with bulges in their jackets don't need to speak English," Shelley said.

"So how did somebody clear the people out?" Jane asked.

"The county zoning people relocated them. The drug dealers were taken to jail, their 'clients' were put in halfway houses, and the homeless were taken to shelters. When the thugs came back, there was nobody to collect from. The county got an offer to buy the place from someone in Romania."

Jane and Shelley exchanged a quick glance. This didn't sound good.

"I assume there's a quitclaim deed somewhere?" Shelley asked. "Does anyone know where it is and if it's valid?"

"The county register of deeds has copies," Bitsy said cheerfully. "I've seen it, and the Realtor, Sandy, and I are all satisfied it's legal."

No mention of a lawyer's opinion in that statement, Jane noted.

Shelley went on opening doors without further comment. Jane took over on the other side of the hall. In one heavily used area, the crummy vinyl had been worn clear through, and a glimpse of a once-nice floral-patterned carpet showed through. Jane wondered idly why anybody would tack down what was probably stolen vinyl flooring over the carpet. Had one of the supposed owners considered renovating it someday? It seemed that someone had wanted to protect the carpet. *How very odd,* Jane thought.

The doorway where the carpet showed turned out to be the only bathroom on the floor. Inside, there was a disgusting pair of toilets without a barrier between them, one chipped and filthy sink, and an equally revolting shower that was almost entirely black with mildew.

Jane looked at Bitsy. "This really should have been torn down. There's no way you can restore this house. Frankly, I'm surprised it wasn't condemned as unfit for human habitation and demolished. It isn't even structurally sound, I'd guess."

This didn't faze Bitsy. "Come on down the stairs and go back up the other side where the work is under way."

Feeling enormously depressed by the sight of a dilapidated house that must have been grand in its heyday, Jane dragged herself along behind Bitsy. Shelley followed, just as disappointed.

As they reached the head of the stairway to the left side of the entryway, they could immediately see the difference. It was a huge area. All the room partitions had been removed. The vinyl flooring had been ripped up. If there had been carpet here, it had also been taken up. Good hardwood floors were still scarred with nail holes. There were windows all around the perimeter letting sunshine in. Most of the framing had been done. Piles of Sheetrock were stacked in the far corner, ready to be put up. Some of it had already been installed.

Two guys were running some lumber through a planer. Bright shiny aluminum duct work for heating and cooling was all in place and glittered in the sun. Thick bunches of electrical wires covered with white coating snaked to the spots where there would be overhead lights and sockets galore.

"This must have been twice the size of the other half," Jane said, shouting over the noise.

"Nope," Bitsy yelled back. "Exactly the same. Isn't it astonishing how large it is when it's opened up? The part at the far end is the master bedroom. His and her bathrooms on either side. The front one will have a hot tub and big overhead windows. The area at this end will be divided by a low partition of bookshelves into a living room on the farther side and a small utility kitchen and bar where we're standing. There will be two small bedrooms nearer the stairs for people who bring along assistants or an au pair."

"Will the other side of the house be the same, but backwards?" Shelley asked.

Bitsy nodded.

"Do you want them to have the same decor?"

"Oh, no," Betsy replied. "Some visitors may stay two or three times. I'd like the two suites to be quite different in style."

"What styles?" Shelley asked.

"Well, that will be partly up to you two. But I picture this one sort of Old Englishy. Big deep claw-footed bathtub, heavily canopied bed with lots of pillows with shams. Floral drapes. Deep, lush carpeting with a subtle pattern. Not too feminine, though. Antique furnishings."

Shelley nodded knowingly. "And the other?"

"I've been thinking of something just a hint retro, do you see? Those big white tiles with the little black ones in the corners in the bathrooms. Curved dividers. A classy 1930s sparse but expensive look. Sort of like those Poirot mysteries on television."

"That's a look that's popular right now," Shelley said, "but I don't think it's going to last much longer. I think you'd make a better investment if you went with something less trendy. So many offices these days are done in that sparse, sterile look. People who work in them don't want to live in them, too. Especially not when they're traveling."

Bitsy was nodding enthusiastically. "I *knew* I'd picked just the right people!"

Jane had to turn away and pretend to examine the piles of Sheetrock to conceal her laughter. Shelley was talking off the top of her head—quite impressively, to be sure—but without any experience in sparse decor. Except the time they saw a house decorated that way and Shelley expressed her hatred of the style.

She was still trying not to laugh when Shelley said, "Jane, we must get on with our measurements."

"There's really no need—" Bitsy began.

Shelley quelled Bitsy with The Look.

The sound of the planer stopped with a gentle moan and Bitsy recovered enough to say, "Let me introduce you to Jack and Henry, our head carpenters on the project."

These two individuals, hearing their names, put down the wood they'd been working on and approached. The taller, burlier, and darker of them put out a sturdy hand to shake theirs and said, "Henrietta Smith at your service." She nearly crushed their hands when she did so.

"Henry is an excellent carpenter, but drives a hard bargain. Her contract states that I, and any future owners, shall never paint over the woodwork. Jack is fanatic about nail placement and concealment. We're really lucky to have them."

Jack, who was short with curly blond hair and lovely blue eyes, extended a small hand and said, "Jacqueline Hunt."

Bitsy said, "These are our decorators, we hope. Shelley Nowack and Jane Jeffry. I know they're going to come to appreciate your fine work as much as Sandy and I do."

"If you don't mind our being in the way, we need to take some measurements," Shelley said with a blinding smile.

"Go right ahead. We're going to take our morning break. You can have this area to yourselves for a while," Henry boomed. She hoisted a thermal cooler, set it on her shoulder, and strode away with Jack following.

"I'll let you get on with it," Bitsy said. "I'll get the contracts and have them downstairs for you when you're finished."

It took a full hour on their hands and knees and climbing ladders to measure down to an eighth of an inch to complete their data on the big open area and a little less than two hours to measure the other side of the house.

Shelley put a thumbtack in the center of each doorway on the other side of the house to take into account the flimsy walls of the tiny rooms that would be coming down eventually. Then they went downstairs and spent another quarter hour measuring the ground-floor rooms. Jane acted as holder of the far end of the metal tape and the recorder of the information in a notebook Shelley had brought along. Shelley herself determined the measurement.

"We're both filthy," Jane said when they were done. "Let's go home and get showers, tidy up, and look over the contracts over lunch."

"I think it's going to take a long soak in the tub," Shelley said, brushing sawdust off the knees of her stylish jeans. "And don't let me forget to get the architectural drawings."

6

It was nearly two-thirty in the afternoon before the two women were cleaned up enough to go to lunch. Jane had staved off her hunger with a handful of Cheez-Its and brushed her teeth afterward to hide the evidence that she hadn't been able to tough it out.

Most of their favorite restaurants were open for lunch and dinner but closed for the afternoon. So they tried a buffet they knew perfectly well they wouldn't like.

"Buffets are all grease and starch but no salt. Inhabited solely by the elderly," Shelley said.

"You can ask for salt," Jane said. "It's a safe place to go with almost no danger of running into young to middle-aged feminists who might overhear our conversation."

Shelley rushed through the line, getting only soup and a roll. Jane dawdled over everything and finally ended up with macaroni and cheese with a side salad and overcooked green beans. It took her a while to find Shelley, who had the contract from Bitsy in front of her face. Meanwhile, she wandered all over the place, nearly losing her grip on the tray several times as she tripped over walkers, crutches, and oxygen containers on little trolleys some of the older customers had left in the aisles.

Shelley made a semi-ladylike snort as Jane sat down.

"You ate before we came, didn't you?" Jane asked.

"Just a soda and a few crackers," Shelley responded. "Oh, no."

"What's the 'oh, no' about?"

"Wait till you read through this. Didn't you bring your own copy along?"

"I forgot," Jane admitted as she pushed a suspicious-looking bean to the side of her plate. It looked as if it might have already been chewed. "Is the contract awful?"

"It's probably fixable, and if it isn't . . ."

Shelley put the papers down and gazed at Jane for the rest of the sentence.

". . . we don't really care if we take the job or not. Right?"

"Right."

"So tell me the worst," Jane went on.

"The payment, of course. She's offering us three percent over our cost. That's ridiculous."

"It might not be in this particular business."

"Jane, you've told me before that writers pay agents ten to fifteen percent. And after we took that botany class I looked up a bunch of stuff on the Internet. Do you know that plant breeders who want someone to promote and sell their flowers and vegetables often pay as much as forty percent the first year? So three percent is peanuts. A downright insult."

"So what do we ask for?"

"Why not twenty-five percent?" Shelley said with a grin. "And be willing to come down to—oh, maybe twenty. Maybe even seventeen and half?"

"What's this stuff going to cost?" Jane asked.

"Thousands and thousands of dollars. Have you priced wallpaper recently?"

"To my sorrow, yes. My disastrous front hall. Remember? And it was so dark when it went up on the wall that I had to buy a very expensive light fixture that would take a hundred-and-fifty-watt bulb without burning down the house."

"We'll have to have a hefty advance," Shelley continued, not even mentioning the outrageous figure it had cost to recarpet her guest room in a good Berber.

"According to this silly contract," she went on,

"we're to be reimbursed for the goods and our fee is paid on the first of every month. That's unacceptable. We need a good five thousand dollars up front. And then there's this other clause that'll make you laugh. If we provide something unacceptable, we have to take it back ourselves. No way. Imagine having a sofa delivered and having to cram it back in my minivan, or pay someone to haul it away?"

"But won't Bitsy go see the choices we've made beforehand? The ultimate decisions should be hers."

"Nope. Except for paint chips, fabric samples, and such that we can bring to the project site. We're to provide digital pictures of everything big. At our own expense. Do you know what a digital camera costs?"

"But you already have one, don't you?"

"I do," Shelley said with indignation. "But that's not something Bitsy knows. Why should she assume we're willing to invest in one for her convenience?"

"On the whole, I don't like this," Jane said. "I never have."

"I'm not crazy about the idea, I have to admit," Shelley said. "But we have nothing to lose by upping the ante. If she turns down our demands, we're home free and haven't lost anything but a little of our time. If she caves, we stand to have some fun out of shopping for this stuff and make tons of money for the pleasure. Jane, we have the upper hand here. That's what we have to keep in mind. This is just a first-try contract, to find out if we're stupid enough to accept it. But we're neither stupid nor desperate. And we've got time on our side."

"Why?"

"She won't be ready for furniture for months. Gives us lots of days to just hang out watching the work, pretending to take notes, deciding if we want to do this, while the clock is ticking for Bitsy. Sooner or later, she'll have to agree to our terms or look for someone else. Or, God help her, do the shopping herself."

Jane pushed her plate toward the side of the table and sighed. When Shelley got the bit in her teeth, there was no stopping her.

Shelly took a sip of her soup. "Ugh. It's awful and it's cold already. Let's go home and maybe we can get together this evening after you've read through this carefully."

Jane was happy to abandon her choices of food as well. The macaroni and cheese must have been made from dried skim milk and the cheapest artificial cheese it was possible to purchase.

After she had fixed Todd, Katie, and herself a good dinner, Jane told the kids to load up the dishwasher and put away the leftovers. Then she went to her bedroom to study the contract. She was as disappointed as Shelley had been. The terms weren't good. What was more, it wasn't even written properly. There were words spelled wrong. Some of the conditions weren't even stated in full sentences. Bitsy had apparently pieced this up herself with no guide at all. And she didn't even know the difference between *it's* and *its*. All of the pronouns were feminine gender.

Jane wasn't normally a fanatic grammar cop, but the contract made her wonder if Bitsy wasn't downright stupid. Or simply too stingy to consult an attorney to draw up a contract.

Either choice was scary.

As she reached for the phone to call Shelley, it rang.

"Have you read it yet?" Shelley asked.

"It's awful. There are sentence fragments about important things that don't even make sense," Jane said.

"That's not all that's wrong," Shelley said. "May I come over and show you something else I've discovered?"

Shelley turned up minutes later with wads and rolls of paperwork. She had fire in her eyes. Even her hair was in disarray, as if she'd been trying to tear bits of it out.

"Wait till you get a look at this." She unrolled the old floor plans as the house had been originally on Jane's kitchen table, and kept them from snapping back into a roll with a salt-and-pepper shaker.

Then she flipped open her notebook. She pointed to the total dimensions of the back of the house on the second floor in the plans. Then she showed Jane her own figures.

"It's a foot and half off. Where did we go wrong?" Jane asked.

"Jane, get a grip. *We* didn't go wrong. You can't have already forgotten how obsessively precise I was upstairs, could you?"

"I'll never forget."

"Didn't Bitsy say this was done by an architectural engineer?"

"I seem to remember that she did."

"Do you see the name of the firm anywhere on this paper? Much less an individual's name?"

Jane stared. "Who really did this? Not Bitsy. She wouldn't even take the time to fake this up, however incompetently."

"Now look at the finished plan for the first floor," Shelley said, removing the salt-and-pepper shaker and replacing the old plan with the new plan and anchoring them down the same way.

Jane read the dimensions, then consulted Shelley's notebook. "It's even farther off what we measured. Nearly three feet just across the back. And no name on this one, either."

"So we figure Bitsy didn't do this herself, right? So who did?"

"Sandy," Jane said firmly.

"Sandra, or some amateur friend of Sandra's, maybe," Shelley qualified. "One of her feminist gang, I'm willing to bet. Maybe she has a daughter studying architecture."

"Shelley, we really should tell Bitsy this. She's not

one of my favorite people, but I hate to see her being made a fool of."

"You bet we will."

Jane thought for a moment, then said, "Shouldn't we just bow out and let them fumble through it themselves?"

"Jane, I've never heard you say a single cowardly thing," Shelley exclaimed.

"Oh, of course you have," Jane said with a laugh.

"Maybe once or twice," Shelley admitted. "But this is serious. Someone's ripping off a stupid woman. One, I admit, who never should have taken on something she knew so little about, but still, neither of us would ever feel good about ourselves again if we didn't at least try to warn Bitsy."

Jane sighed. "You're right. Damn."

7

Jane and Shelley showed up early the next morning, ready to pull poor Bitsy aside and point out the errors in the drawing. This time the street in front was even more crowded. As they got out of Shelley's van, a siren screamed and an ambulance pulled into the front yard.

"What's happened?" Jane asked, realizing it was a stupid question to ask Shelley, who was as surprised and alarmed as she was.

Bitsy and Sandra were standing on the sidewalk, wringing their hands. Sandra looked confused and was clutching her ever-present purse to her chest. Bitsy was clearly angry.

"What's going on?" Shelley asked as Jane caught a glimpse of two well-dressed middle-aged women she'd never seen bending over and vomiting in what the plans had shown as a bank of azaleas that would be in front of the porch.

"Since it's a chilly morning, our furnace guy tried out the system and within moments there was the most *awful* smell," Bitsy said.

"I have to go tend to your friends Dorothea and Wendy," Sandra said, indicating the women who were where the azaleas would someday make their appearance. They were now being tended by the ambulance attendants. A breeze sprung up and suddenly Jane and Shelley could smell it as well. Something terribly rotten and utterly disgusting made them hold their hands over their noses and mouths.

When the wind changed direction, Jane said to Bitsy, "Your furnace guy? I thought all the workers were women."

"Not quite all. But Wesley Woodley's an exception. He works for a company run by a woman. Ms. Betty Stanley. You may have heard of her. She's in a lot of civic organizations."

"Did I hear my name being used in vain?" a very tall young man asked.

"Wesley!" Bitsy yelped. "What is that smell?"

Wesley shrugged. "I couldn't go in the house to tell. Mrs. Stanley's bringing some breathing apparatus so I can find out. Did anyone have the wits to turn off the furnace?"

"I didn't," Bitsy admitted.

"That's the first thing I need to do. Second, you need to rent some powerful fans to clear the odor out."

"Where do you rent fans?" Bitsy asked.

"Ask your contractor," he replied. Jane thought there was a hint of a sneer in his remark, but couldn't be sure. Unless he had had a run-in with Bitsy before, it was a logical question for an ordinary person to ask. Jane herself would have had to ask.

The ambulance people had moved the women who were ill away from the house and put them on blankets on the ground with damp cloths over their faces, and were taking their blood pressures.

Jane approached Sandra and asked, "How are they? And who are they?"

"Friends of Bitsy's she wanted to show the house to," Sandra said with irritation, fidgeting with the strap of her purse. "I wish she'd picked any other day. The nurse in the van says since they didn't ingest anything and it only smelled like something rotten, not chemical, they'll probably be okay. But someone has to drive them to the hospital to confirm whether it was dangerous fumes."

Jane knew what Sandra *really* meant. That she and Shelley had nothing better to do. "Weren't other people in the house? And they might have felt like gagging, but no one else is sick, are they?"

"I don't imagine you're free to . . . ?"

"No. Shelley and I were on our way to an appointment." After a moment's thought, she added, "To see an attorney about Bitsy's contract. I suppose since they're Bitsy's friends, hauling them to the hospital is her job," Jane said.

"I guess so. But she really needs to be here."

"Who needs to be here, Sandy?" Bitsy asked, approaching the two.

Jane got as far from them as fast as she could. "Shelley, let's hide out for a bit," she said, grabbing Shelley's arm. "Sandra and Bitsy are trying to figure out how they can shove the responsibility for taking those two women to the hospital on us."

"I'm not letting strangers I didn't invite over here, and probably stink for a number of reasons, ride in my van," Shelley said. Jane's first thought was how callous this sounded, but she realized that quite honestly, she'd feel the same way.

"Let's go and have breakfast somewhere if you're up to it. I need a cup of coffee to get the smell out of my head."

There was a pricey coffeehouse a block or two away, and as they sat down with their cups and the pastries they couldn't resist, Shelley said, "I guess we'd better wait awhile to hit Bitsy with more bad news."

"I don't know," Jane said with a wicked grin. "It might be interesting to see how much she can take before she crumbles."

Shelley laughed so hard, she almost snorted coffee up her nose.

When she'd recovered, Jane asked, "What do you think caused that odor?"

"One thing it isn't is a body," Shelley said. "It wouldn't fit in a furnace or a duct. It could be just a dead animal that already was awfully ripe, and turning on the blower created a crisis."

They dawdled just long enough to be present at the renovation site when Wesley, in protective gear and what looked like a World War I–era gas mask unearthed from Mrs. Stanley's attic, reappeared with a heavyweight plastic bag at the front door. He removed the gas mask.

"Someone shoved a wad of frozen shrimp way back into one of the ducts," he shouted across the yard at Bitsy. "You're going to have to find a way of disposing of it."

"Put it in the Dumpster," Bitsy yelled back. She had already either delivered her friends home or forced someone else to do so. Come to think of it, Jane decided, the ambulance people should have taken them along to the hospital. Apparently the women didn't want to make any more fuss.

"No, the bag will probably explode." Wesley set it down on the lawn and came over to them. Jane and Shelley got close enough to overhear the conversation, but not so close that they could smell him. Sandra and Bitsy moved around a bit to get Wesley downwind of them.

"I had to tear a lot of the duct work out to find it," Wesley complained. "And the smell is just as bad as ever. You'll have to call in someone to deodorize the whole house."

"There are people who do that?" Bitsy said with awe. "What will that cost?"

"I have no idea," Wesley said. This time the contempt in his voice was clear. "And those fans that are coming off that truck next door aren't strong enough. You must air the house out thoroughly first. The stench is in the wood and the Sheetrock. It'll all have to be treated. While it's being done, you need to secure the property."

"Secure the property?" Bitsy was at sea. Apparently she thought this was a financial term. "What will that cost me?"

"It means put new locks on the doors and replace the crumbling plywood in the open windows." Wesley was openly sneering now. "Anyone could, and has, gotten in here to commit this act of vandalism."

Standing where they were on the sidewalk, Jane and Shelley heard the purr of a car and turned to see an enormous black stretch limo stop in front with no regard to the fact that it was blocking traffic. The chauffeur came around and opened the back door, and an extremely well-dressed middle-aged man with a full and beautifully cut head of pure white hair stepped out.

He approached, saying, "Bitsy, dear, I was doing some business in the neighborhood and saw everyone standing outside. What's going on?" He would have been quite handsome if he hadn't been smirking.

Bitsy's face hardened. "Neville. How coincidental that you are here. Something tells me you know exactly what's going on."

The man looked genuinely surprised. Or maybe it was a good act, Jane thought.

"How would I know what you're up to? Is this a picnic of some sort?"

"Neville, go away. You're not welcome here," Bitsy said and turned her back on him.

Grinning again, he approached Jane and Shelley. "What do you ladies do? Stencil cute little designs around the tops of the rooms? I'm Bitsy's ex-husband. The man whose hard-earned money is financing this idiocy. Much against my will, I might say."

Before Shelley could draw breath to tell him off, Betsy screamed, "Neville, leave my friends alone. If you don't get out of here this instant, I'm calling the police."

He bowed to her with mock respect and turned and slowly, arrogantly, let his driver open the door for him. "Have fun, dear," he said before it closed.

Bitsy actually stomped her feet like a child getting ready to have a tantrum.

Jane and Shelley strolled away. "She's tougher than I suspected," Jane said, chuckling. "I don't think this is the day we want to put her over the edge."

8

When Jane and Shelley returned home, Shelley said, "I think we ought to just stay away until the stink's gone."

"Okay by me. There's no rush," Jane replied.

"It'll give me time to write up a new contract," Shelley said.

"You're starting over?"

"From scratch. It's going to be a big job to rekey the whole thing into the computer. Making it fair is only one part. Trying to figure out how to make the sentence fragments make sense is another, and the third is correcting the grammar and spelling."

"Better you than me," Jane said with relief.

After Shelley went home to start her project, Jane

checked the answering machine and found a message to call Todd's math teacher, Miss Milton. That was ominous. She returned the call and was told the teacher was in class, but would call back on her break. When Miss Milton called, she wouldn't commit to what she had to say without a face-to-face meeting. They set it up for immediately after school that afternoon.

Jane did a couple of loads of laundry. Up and down the basement stairs. When all the kids were gone, she was going to convert their bathroom upstairs to a laundry room. Clothes tended to lie neglected in the basement. And they often came up smelling ever so slightly of kitty litter in the winter, when Max and Meow didn't go outside much.

What on earth was the teacher after her for? she wondered as she sorted darks from lights and came up with too many darks for one load and too few lights for a full load. Todd's best grades had always been in math. That wasn't saying much. They were usually Bs and the rest were Cs. And the way he was actually staying his room in the evenings and actually studying . . . it couldn't be terrible news, could it?

Jane hadn't met this teacher yet. School had started only a short time ago, and the dreaded parents' night when they had to sit in little chairs and be bored senseless hadn't occurred yet. But when Jane found the room, the chairs and tables were normal size for the older kids. The teacher met her with a smile as they introduced themselves.

"Mrs. Jeffry, I'm sorry to inconvenience you this way, but did you hear about our testing this year?" Meeting a blank look, she went on, "We don't normally test first thing, but this year we wanted to get a handle on what we were up against. There's a movement to give vouchers for private schools when the public ones don't perform as well as they should."

"I do know that," Jane said pleasantly. She'd expected a Miss Milton to be straight out of college, but the woman was nearly Jane's age.

"This school district isn't in any danger, mind. But the school board decided to test first thing this year and again at the end of the year, and see what sort of improvement was made."

"I see," Jane said, wondering when Miss Milton would get to the point.

"This is a national test. I forgot to say that up front. And your Todd tested into the high ninety-ninth percentile."

Jane was too astonished to speak for a moment. "Are you sure of that?" she finally managed to ask.

Miss Milton nodded. "It's a remarkable skill that he's never shown. His previous scores in past years on the same sort of test put him in the upper sixtieth percentile. That's good, of course. But we have no idea why this great leap of skill happened."

"He went a few weeks to that half-day summer school the district set up," Jane said, "but didn't seem to enjoy anything but the math class. And he's become unusually studious this year. He's never really cared what kind of grades he gets, but seems to have turned a corner. Hormones, maybe," Jane finished with a smile.

"You're sure that's it?"

The smile faded. "Excuse me, Miss Milton. You're not suggesting that Todd cheated, are you?"

"I'm not suggesting it at all, but I'm forced to ask when there's such a remarkable difference."

"When was this test taken?" Jane asked.

Miss Milton told her date.

"I've got my datebook in the car. Let me get it."

When Jane returned, she had the datebook open to the week in question. "Monday he did his social studies homework right after school and was allowed to go to a seven o'clock showing of a movie. I picked him up. Here's the note of the time I was to be there," she said, pointing to the entry. "It's not noted here, but he came home, watched a television program with me about some sort of little furry African animals I've forgotten the name of, and went to bed with the lights out."

"So he wasn't memorizing something late into the night?"

"Certainly not."

"Mrs. Jeffry, I'm sorry I had to ask. Todd is a nice boy and you have a reputation for raising bright children. I've checked Mike's and Katie's records. I'm simply required to confirm that he's actually made this improvement."

"Miss Milton, Todd's always been a lazy student.

He's very bright about things he wants to be bright about. But it's too easy to slide by with a B average. I think I can promise you there was no cheating done."

"Mrs. Jeffry, I believe you a hundred percent. As I said, I'm required to ask."

Good news, bad vibes, Jane thought as she drove home. With a bit of the third child syndrome thrown in. Had she failed Todd? Was there the slightest chance he would cheat? No.

She stopped at Shelley's house before going home. "Sorry to interrupt you, but I want to tell you something," Jane said. She recounted the conversation with the teacher.

"How outrageous!" Shelley exploded. "Todd? Todd cheat? No way, Jane."

"He's always been the quietest and most self-sufficient of my kids," Jane said. "I didn't have to badger and nag him as I did Mike and am still doing with Katie. Have I completely misjudged him? Have I accidentally neglected him?"

"I'd like to slap you upside the head for even saying that," Shelley said. "Of course not. How many of his soccer games have you sat through, even though soccer bores you senseless? How much did you spend on Legos when he was only interested in them? You didn't leave the house for a full week when he had his tonsils out. He told my son that you treated him like a baby and nearly drove him crazy bringing him Jell-O and soft drinks. You've driven him all over the place for camps. You've done the room-mother thing for him. He's a thoroughly nice kid. Just quiet and self-contained compared to your older kids. Come to think of it, I'd rather slap that teacher upside the head instead for even putting the thought in your mind."

"I would, too. But she was right. When a kid improves that dramatically, it could be a good sign or a sign of cheating. She had to ask. I don't blame her. She hardly knows him and she'd never met me."

"Then I'll put off beating her up," Shelley said with a grin. "You've just raised a mathematical genius and neither he nor you knew it until now. You've said he's taking school seriously this year. This score is the pay-off, Jane. Just go home and praise him."

"Thanks, Shelley. Maybe I did need that metaphorical slap."

Jane went home and thought a little more about it. There's nothing worse for a single parent—maybe *any* parent—than to think a child has been ignored or neglected, but Shelley was right. She'd done right by Todd. He just wasn't as blabby as the others. He didn't even talk much until he was practically two years old. But he watched and listened to everything with interest.

When he became older, he was obsessed for several years with Legos. Then he left that behind, put all the little pieces, hundreds of them, in a box still stored in the basement, and lived for soccer. But without explanation, he hadn't even joined a team last summer. He'd left soccer behind for math. He made the decision himself, as he usually did. That was a good thing. Showed a sense of purpose. A willingness to take on a new obsession.

She went upstairs to hunt him down to compliment him for his score, but he had the first word. "Mom, can you help me work out something on your computer?"

"What's that?"

He showed her a big chart he was creating. "This isn't a good way to do it. I'd have to copy it over and over again."

The sheet had a hand-drawn grid. Each square had a number. Some of the numbers were circled. "What is this?" Jane asked. "Oh, wait. I think I might know."

"It's about prime numbers. Do you know what they are?" Todd asked.

"Of course I do. They're the numbers like seven and eleven that can't be evenly divided by other numbers."

Todd was surprised. "So I was reading something this summer about prime numbers. Nobody's ever found a pattern for them. The larger they get, the fewer there are."

"That's right. They get so many new divisors."

"Right. So there must still be a pattern of some kind. Maybe it's a spiral, maybe a long rectangle. Maybe the pattern goes from high to low. See why I need to do this on a computer?"

Jane nodded. "So you can list a whole lot of them, mark the primes, and rearrange them."

Todd stared at her. "Gosh, Mom. I didn't know you knew about this kind of stuff."

"I liked math when I was your age, come to think of it. And before you kids were born I did the book-keeping for the Jeffry family pharmacy."

"So could we move your computer out of the base-ment? I hate it down there. Maybe we could set it up in the living room."

"How about the dining room? We don't use it as often. Better yet, why don't we get you your own com-puter and you can help me move mine to my bedroom."

His eyes lit up like beacons. "You'd really do that? Buy me a computer? All my own?"

"It's an investment in your future, kiddo. Who knows, you might turn into another Einstein and sup-port me in my old age. Now, what I came up here to tell you about it this. I had a talk with your math teacher this afternoon. You know that test you took at the beginning of school? "

"The math and language one? Yeah?"

"You're over the ninety-ninth percentile in math."

"Way cool! I'll bet the teacher thought I cheated."

"No, of course she didn't," Jane said. "Let's go buy some computer magazines before I have to fix dinner and see what's the best deal. But no modem. I don't want you roaming the Internet. There's a lot of nasty stuff there."

Todd rolled his eyes. "Mom, we have computers at school that block that stuff. You can do that yourself if you don't trust me. But there's got to be a lot of stuff on the Internet about prime numbers. You don't want me to reinvent the wheel, do you?"

"As much as I'll eventually regret saying this, Todd, you're right."

9

Jane spent the next two days studying computer magazines and making notes of costs and features. She and Todd went out both evenings looking them over. He was remarkably patient with her for being so thorough, especially because she had to keep asking clerks to remind what the difference was between RAM and ROM. Todd knew which side his bread was buttered on and kept out of the discussion.

Jane was astonished to learn how little a computer costs these days. She had an old, slow one that she'd bought in a fit of pique one summer when the kids were driving her crazy and someone at the bank convinced her she needed it to do her budget. She'd paid at least four times what they cost now.

Jane couldn't quite believe she was doing this. She'd been so parsimonious for so long until that summer, when she'd had a bit of an epiphany when she broke her foot and decided she really didn't have to behave as a pauper. The kids had their college funds set up. Her house had been paid off by her late husband's life insurance policy. Computers were necessary for kids now. And a better one was a justifiable purchase for her. She didn't need a new monitor or printer, so hers would be cheaper than Todd's.

She didn't even spot Shelley those two days. She assumed Shelley must have been busy redoing the contract, which was as close as she got to thinking about Bitsy's house renovation.

Finally she called her Uncle Jim early on Saturday morning. He worked for the Chicago police force and was far more knowledgeable about computers than she was. Jim was only an honorary uncle, an old friend of her family.

Jane said, "Uncle Jim, tell me what kind of computer to get. Don't explain why, please. I'm overloaded with information I don't understand. Just tell me brand and model. I'm getting one for Todd and one for myself."

Laughing, Uncle Jim named one. "Want me to load things from your dinosaur on there before you get started?"

"Oh. Can that be done?" She'd been afraid she'd have to completely retype the whole manuscript.

"I'll bring my stand-alone Zip drive and download what you want to keep. The computer you're getting already has an internal one to transfer it to and move it all onto the new one. How about a pork roast with mashed potatoes for dinner at your house tonight? I'll come over early. I'm off duty at two."

"A small price to pay. Thanks, Uncle Jim."

"Why are you getting two?"

"Because Todd and I would fight over a good one. And he needs one of his own."

"Why's that?"

"I'll explain over dinner. Or let Todd explain."

"Okay. Do you remember what I said to get?"

"I think so," Jane said.

"Write this down. Exactly as I say." He made her read it back.

By Saturday at one o'clock, both Jane and Todd had computers in the house, somewhat unpacked and instructions sitting out. Todd, thank goodness, had his desk free since the last hamster died and he got rid of the elaborate cage.

Jane had the roast just starting to warm up when Uncle Jim arrived.

"Janey, darlin', your house smells so good. Did you get the computers I told you to?"

"Would I ask advice and ignore it? Five o'clock and the food will be on the table."

Jim had Todd's computer ready to go and Jane's new one set up on her desk and running as she set the last part of the meal, the salad, on the dining room table.

"Mom, may I take my plate upstairs?" Todd asked.

Jane looked to Uncle Jim for approval. He nodded and said, "But don't spill anything on the keyboard."

Todd, to Jane's relief, didn't make a face or mention that this warning was obvious.

"So what's this all about, Janey?" he said when Todd was gone.

She explained about Todd's amazing math score and the prime number deal. She didn't get into the teacher's suspicions. No reason to upset him. He'd have been even madder than Shelley had been.

"I'm glad you've done this for him. And for yourself. You've always been too damned stingy with yourself. I guess the Jeffry pharmacies are going well. I saw another new one on my way over."

"They're making money hand over fist. I almost feel guilty about my share of the money. I don't do any of the work."

"But that was the deal when you used that inheritance of yours to bail them out when they were about to go under, wasn't it? And the one good thing your husband did was to insist you'd get his third share forever as part of the deal."

"He didn't exactly mean to die and leave it to me," Jane said. "But I'm glad it was written that way. And it's finally allowed me to get the college funds set up and spend a bit on myself."

"It must break Thelma's heart," Jim said, rubbing his hands together. He'd harbored a strong dislike for Jane's mother-in-law for decades.

"I'm not so sure. Steve's brother Ted's wife, Dixie, still hasn't had the baby they so desperately want, and Thelma's crazy about grandchildren. Not so crazy about me, though. I think if I hadn't had the kids when Steve died, she'd have tried to contest the contract."

"She wouldn't have gotten anywhere with that," Jim said. Changing the subject, he asked, "So how are your folks doing in Denmark?"

"They must be fine," Jane said. "I haven't had an E-mail from them for the last week. This trip is just a vacation. Not a diplomacy job."

"Speaking of jobs, how are you filling your free time?" Jim asked.

Jane laughed. "You wouldn't believe what Shelley's trying to get us into. A feminist home renovation. Don't look at me like that, Uncle Jim. We haven't agreed to do it yet. Shelley's rewriting the contract they offered us and really jacking up the perks."

"What in the world do the two of you know about renovating?"

"We're just to be the decorators."

Jane explained about Bitsy and her influx of money. About Sandy. About Jack and Henry. With a couple of days of not thinking about it, it seemed outrageously funny even to her. But when she got to the story of the spoiled shrimp in the air ducts, Jim asked, "Did anyone 'fess up?"

"Nope. Not that I know of. The furnace guy who'd done the duct work was furious."

"Of course he was. Was it some idiot's idea of a joke or sabotage?" Jim asked.

"I don't know. Bitsy thinks her ex-husband is responsible. That must have been one of the nastiest divorces in history. Aside from a few of Henry the Eighth's that come to mind."

"I'd be careful of taking this job if I were you," Jim said. "I don't want to overstep my bounds, but that's my advice."

"I think I agree. The contract we were given wasn't even grammatical. And Shelley says it's outrageously stingy. But if she can put over the one she's working on, it could be fun for us and very profitable."

"I thought you were just talking about already being financially comfortable."

"Comfortable. Just barely. But who in their right mind wouldn't like a bit more money to spend?"

"You don't say that with conviction," Uncle Jim said with a smile. "Cough up what this is really about."

"It'll sound silly to you. You have a job. But, Uncle Jim, my job has always been to raise my kids to be independent when they're grown, and I'm almost there. Katie will go to college next year and Todd a couple of years later. I've had my full share of club and volunteer work. I don't want to turn into one of those women who consider bridge night or bingo tournaments with a bunch of their peers the highlight of the week."

Uncle Jim patted her hand. "I do understand, Janey. That's why I'm still plugging away, even though I'm only a desk jockey these days. It isn't the money. It's the pride and challenge of doing something well enough to be paid." He leaned back from the table. "Now, darlin', what's for dessert?"

10

Bright and early Monday morning, Shelley was at Jane's door. "Let's fortify ourselves with a good breakfast and then tackle Bitsy."

"You're doing the tackling, right? I'm just the cheering section. I hope."

"I'll be happy to carry it out, but you have to read my version of the contract first, so you'll know when to cheer."

"Is it really good?"

Shelley pulled herself up into a pillar of indignation. "Of course."

"I really should call Mel first. He left four messages on my phone over the weekend, explaining that he was finishing up the paperwork on a big case and asking me to call him back. But I was so busy, and the times I did call, he was away from his desk. What a romance. Phone tag only. We're both afraid to leave a sexy message for fear someone else will hear it first."

"Busy with what?" Shelley demanded, ignoring Jane's reply.

"Buying computers."

"Plural?"

"One for me and one for Todd."

"Explain this to me on the way. I want your full attention on the contract while we eat. You need to drive. My van is making a funny noise."

Jane was astonished. "You'd ride in my disreputable station wagon? I'd have cleaned it out if I'd known."

"No, you wouldn't have. But I don't care. Just as long as there's somewhere to sit where there aren't bags of birdseed, dry cleaning, or school papers."

Jane explained how she'd spent the weekend. Shelley, flipping through the contract one last time, paid very little attention except to mutter, "Good for you, Jane."

When they reached the restaurant, Shelley said, "Let me order for both of us. I know what you always get. Start reading."

Jane had known Shelley most of her adult life and knew when it was possible to object to her bossiness. This wasn't one of those times.

She applied herself as diligently as she could and hoped she could finish before they were through eating so Shelley could pay their bill while she tried once again to reach Mel.

It wasn't to be. Shelley finished eating first, continually warning Jane not to spill anything on the contract.

"What would it matter?" Jane said, slightly snippily. "You can always print out a fresh one."

"I want to show Bitsy what a well-done, well-presented contract should look like without sticky bun icing smeared on it. And I don't want to go back home to print a new one. Aren't you through yet?"

"With the contract or my breakfast?"

"Both."

Jane sighed, looking longingly at her now-cold second waffle. "I guess I am. Let's go."

When they'd almost reached the construction site, Jane asked, "Do you think they got rid of the smell? I don't want to go in if they haven't."

"We'll see. I'm determined to get Bitsy away from Sandra anyway. We might just ask her to come outside to talk."

"Are you going to make her read the contract right there in front of you?"

"No. That would be tacky."

"It wasn't tacky when you did it to me," Jane said, showing off, as she spoke, how well she could parallel-park on a busy street.

"I'll give her the contract, pointing out, naturally,

how unprofessional hers was. I'll bet you anything Sandra drew it up. Anyway, I'm then going to rat on Sandra about the measured drawings. Just so you know what to expect."

They found Sandra and Bitsy in the end of the upstairs part of the house that was being completed first. Everybody was relieved that the horrible odor was gone. Today two people were starting the Sheetrock. One was obviously a real, genuine male. Everyone watched as he picked up an eight-by-four-foot sheet as if it were no heavier than a piece of paper and heaved it precisely into place.

He turned around and Bitsy said, "Ladies, meet Carl Stringfield. Isn't he a wonder?"

"He is," Jane and Shelley at the same time.

Bitsy told him their names and what they'd be doing as if it were already sorted out and a done deal. "And this is Ev," she said as a lithe young woman with dark curly hair entered the room.

"Bitsy, I've asked you not to call me Ev several times. My name is Evaline Berman. Evaline. Got it? Or Ms. Berman. And who are you ladies?" Her expression of discontent suddenly disappeared as she spotted the newcomers.

"Shelley Nowack and Jane Jeffry," Shelley said, shaking hands with Evaline. "We're thinking of being the decorators." There was the barest hint of emphasis on the word "thinking."

"Evaline is the mud person," Bitsy said with a titter. "Isn't that what you call it, usually?"

"That's what Carl calls it. I call it joint cement."

"She's also an inventor," Bitsy continued. "She has a special sort of joint cement that she's patenting. Dries so fast you wouldn't believe it. Sands easily and most often doesn't even require a second coat."

Jane remembered having the garage Sheetrocked. It took days to dry and made the most awful mess when it was patched and sanded. White powder seeped into virtually everything in her whole house. "That's very impressive," Jane admitted.

Shelley was trying to get Bitsy away. Sandra was roaming around straightening up tools and debris. She wasn't nearly as well dressed today. She had on designer jeans with a nice scoop-neck T-shirt with satiny trim at the throat, but with the usual high heels and the usual purse practically a part of her body.

Shelley finally succeeded in dragging Bitsy off and made a gesture for Jane to follow. But as Jane started to do so, Evaline said, "Could I have a word with you?"

"Sure." Jane was relieved to have an excuse not to be there for the slaughter.

"This is kind of silly of me, but I've asked for half an hour off this morning to go and sign the patent application," Evaline said. "I'd like it to be a bit of a celebration, but I've only recently moved here and don't have anybody I know to be a witness. The attorney's office is just a block or two away. Will you go with me?"

"I can't tell you how happy that would make me," Jane said. Shelley would have a fit, but then again, Shelley might be on such a roll that she wouldn't even notice Jane wasn't there.

Jane reconnoitered. Shelley and Bitsy were in the dining room on the first floor. As she passed, she said, "I'll be right back. Evaline needs some help."

"Wait . . ." Shelley's voice faded away as Jane fled. Evaline drove them in her pickup truck, which was spotless.

It was a joy to see Evaline signing her application. She literally glowed with pride and satisfaction. Jane used her best handwriting and the fountain pen Katie had given her last Christmas. The women hugged when the signing was done. Evaline made a move to hug the attorney as well, but he staved her off with a hearty handshake and a promise to let her know when he heard back from the patent office.

As they started back to the construction site, Evaline said, "That was good of you. I hope it goes okay. There are a lot of other people trying to do what I've done. But I think I have the best formula I know of. I've checked out all the others that are currently on the market. They do dry faster than they used to and the texture is finer than before. But unless luck is against me, I'll be the first to be able to market mine."

"Let me give you my address and telephone number," Jane said, pulling out her checkbook and tearing off a deposit slip. "I've always thought that if I got a real business card, I'd have it designed to make it look like a deposit slip."

Evaline laughed out loud, then said, "Could I ask one more favor? I'm almost out of something I need for the next batch of joint cement. It's from the grocery store. It would take me only a second."

It was less than five minutes, and Evaline had whatever it was wrapped in a large, apparently heavy paper bag that was sealed closed with strong tape. "Don't mean to be secretive with you, but the attorney warned me to be very careful no one else in the world knows what's in this mix."

"That's good advice," Jane replied. "I'm surprised at how comfortable it is to ride in this truck. I'm thinking of getting a new vehicle to replace my elderly station wagon. What I most want is something with good shock absorbers. I always feel like a pea being rattled around in a can in what I've got."

Evaline started the engine and said, "This is the greatest thing I've ever had, and I'll have to keep it in good running condition forever."

As they were pulling out of the grocery store parking lot, another car behind them turned the other way. "Isn't that Sandra?" Jane asked.

"Might be," Evaline said, glancing at the rearview

mirror. "I think her car is a darker blue. But about a million people have a car like that. Come to think of it, half a million have a truck exactly like mine. The first day I parked this baby," she said, patting the front dash, "I came back out and got in the wrong one and said to myself, 'Who in the hell left this crummy coffee cup in my brand-new truck?' before I realized it wasn't mine. That's why I have that tinsel bow on the hood ornament."

"I'd love for that to happen to me. I drive the rattiest old station wagon still on the road," Jane said with a laugh. "And I've never seen one remotely like it."

"I wish we had the time to celebrate in style, but we both need to get back. Maybe a beer after work and some really good pretzels," Evaline said.

"You're on. But only if Shelley doesn't kill me first."

"Why would she?"

"Because I was supposed to stand by and be supportive when she told Bitsy what was wrong with the contract she was offering us."

Evaline grinned. "One of Sandy's contracts, huh? I got one, too. I rewrote it."

"Did that work?" Jane asked.

"Pretty much so. At least I went from being slave labor to contract labor."

"I'm afraid Shelley's is too far from realistic. Maybe that's a good thing."

"I could tell you two weren't nutcases the minute

I met you," Evaline said as they arrived back at the house under construction. "I bet neither of you let her call you by a man's name. Shelley would be Shel, no doubt, but it's hard to make Jane sound butch enough."

11

Apparently Shelley hadn't needed backup and wasn't angry with Jane for running off.

"So how did it go?" Jane screwed up the courage to ask.

"Wonderfully," Shelley said. "I showed Bitsy the errors and conditions of the contract. She started apologizing, saying she shouldn't have turned that over to Sandra to do. Bitsy said she didn't know much about contracts, but at least she did know good English from bad. She was truly indignant about the grammatical errors and misplaced apostrophes."

"And then?" Jane prodded.

"I showed her the house plans," Shelley said. "I was surprised that she realized for the first time without my even saying it that there was no indication of who had done them. Then she asked who'd penciled those other numbers in for the dimensions. I told her it was I. And didn't she remember how annoyingly thorough we were when we took the exact measurements?"

Shelley couldn't have looked more pleased if she'd singlehandedly conquered a whole country.

"I presume you suggested that she fire Sandra?"

Shelley grabbed Jane's hands as if they were girls. "I didn't even get the chance. Can you believe it? She said straight out that Sandra would be gone by tomorrow."

"And how is this job to proceed?" Jane asked. "Bitsy doesn't know enough to be a contractor."

"She said she'd consulted someone else first. A man, though. Sandra heard about it at one of their empowerment meetings."

"Empowerment meetings?" Jane exclaimed.

"You don't want to know," Shelley assured her, releasing Jane's hands as she spoke. "Anyway, Sandra knew about her considering this man, someone named Joe, and said a lot of bad things about him. So Sandra drags Bitsy aside for dinner after the empowerment meeting and does her own cheerleading. Talks about all her own credentials, which may or may not have been true, according to Bitsy."

"She didn't even check them out?" Jane asked.

"She checked one thing and it was wrong because the college Sandra graduated from had no record of her. Bitsy even gave them her married name and they still came up blank, but she put it down to a fouled-up computer program at the college. Bitsy said she got so busy with the plans that she forgot to go back and check any more of the references."

Jane plunged her fingers into her hair in pure frustration at Bitsy's naivete. "I can't believe it!"

"Quit interrupting or I'll lose the thread. Sandy gave her the feminist pitch. It must have turned Bitsy's brains to mush. It was odd, though. Bitsy repeated some of what Sandra said."

"Like what?"

"The domestic angle, apparently. How no matter what the law said, Sandy told her, homes were always women's. They set the schedule, made the meals, hired what help they needed, raised the children, knew instinctively when the dishwasher was making a noise it shouldn't, so the best people to restore the house would be women.

"She surely knew how to play on Bitsy. I could almost sympathize with her for falling for that. But it's so inconsistent with what I believe Sandra really thinks. Isn't that exactly what the far left fringe of feminism wants to get away from? I'd guess that she's never even run a dishwasher because it's a girly thing. Not the least empowering."

Now that Shelley had outlined the gist of the conversation, she returned, as Jane had feared, to another matter. "And just where were you when I was pointing this all out to her?"

"At a patent lawyer's office with Evaline."

Shelley's jaw dropped. "What?"

"She's applying for a patent for her gunk she uses on the Sheetrock. She said she had no close friends to go with her as a witness and since you were obviously busy, would I come along? It was really sort of touching. How could I have turned down a plea like that?"

"I'll accept this. Marginally," Shelley said.

"And we're going to have a beer with her after work."

"What kind of bar? Not one of those peculiar ones, I hope. Bald women bikers with pierced parts?"

"No, it's that neighborhood place that serves barbecue."

They were early, and Jane mentioned that Evaline would most likely want to thank Jane herself by buying the first round of drinks.

"We're not having beer, are we? I have to stagger home and cook dinner," Shelley said.

"I think any drink is fine," Jane said. "Since I'm doing the driving, I'll have a soft drink. It might make the ride home a little mellower."

Evaline waved at them from the door and approached. "This is on me. What do you ladies want?"

"Do they have cold bottled water here?" Shelley asked.

With a laugh, Evaline said, "I'll ask. What for you, Jane?"

Jane said, "An RC if they have it. Otherwise, whatever you think."

Evaline was back a few minutes later carrying their drinks on a tray. A can of RC Cola for Jane, a bottle of cold water for Shelley, and a root beer foaming in a frosty mug for herself.

"You're not a part-time waitress here, are you?" Shelley asked.

"No, but I've waited my share of tables."

"Jane said you're relatively new to Chicago," Shelley prodded.

"I've been here about nine months. But too busy to get to know much of anyone. I inadvertently chose an apartment where most of the others are elderly women who eye my boots, jeans, and truck with deep suspicion. Haven't had time to find a more congenial space to live."

"Where did you grow up?" Jane asked.

"All over Michigan," Evaline said. "In foster homes."

"Oh, I'm so sorry. I didn't mean to pry," Jane said.

Evaline pushed back her curly hair with an immaculately clean hand with practical short nails and said, "It's not prying. Most of it wasn't as bad as you hear. I was very lucky to spend several years with good people. The man was an English professor and the woman taught high school chemistry. They were in their forties and had no children, so they took me in. I was about eleven then. My mother had died of drink. And no one knew who my other relatives were. This couple treated me well. I learned good English and had chemistry forced on me. Luckily, I came to find it interesting."

"Did you spend a long time with them?" Shelley asked.

"Almost three years. Then the thing they most wanted in the world finally happened. The wife got pregnant long after they'd given up on ever having children of their own. I stuck around until the baby, a cute, fat little boy, was born. But it was obvious that they'd lost all interest in me. Understandable, of course. After six months I was just an unpaid babysitter, so I was moved around to lots of other people."

"Nice people, I hope," Jane said.

Evaline shrugged. "Not many of them were. They were just in the game to make a little money, most of them. But because of the people I'd been with first, I realized I was tons smarter than most of the foster parents and the mobs of kids they kept. I was able to buffalo them. I think I downright scared some of them. When I got out of the welfare system, I decided I didn't much want to be surrounded by kids and housewives cashing in on the social services. So with the money I'd saved from waiting tables, babysitting, and doing chemistry papers for the high school kids—that was really profitable—I went to trade school to learn a craft.

"Learned all about electrical stuff first, which bored

me senseless and frightened me as well," Evaline went on. "Then I tried carpentry, but didn't have a gift for it. And it requires an awful lot of expensive equipment, even if you do love doing it."

"How did you come to being interested in Sheetrocking?"

"Someone desperate hired me to sand. Everybody in the construction business hates that part. I figured it was well-paying work, but soon realized why it's hard to get anyone to do it. It's not the Sheetrock that's hard to put up. Just takes accurate numbers and lots of muscle. The studs are there. It's easy to measure and cut. It's all just numbers. But the sanding part is a nightmare. Plain hard work that has to be done twice. The dust gets in your eyes, nose, and hair, and it leaves a trail of white dust all over your belongings."

"I'll bet that's when you started thinking back to your chemistry," Jane said.

Evaline smiled. "Precisely. I spent all my free evenings in the library at the computer learning everything there is to learn about every kind of mortar. I'm boring you, aren't I?" she said with a laugh.

"Not at all," Jane said. "I'm fascinated by the inside dope on why people choose what they do with their lives."

Evaline grinned and went on. "To make a long story short—well, a bit shorter—I was cruising the Internet for old structures that are still standing and suddenly discovered something stunning."

"What was that?" Shelley asked.

"Unfortunately, my attorney told me never to reveal it. But I moved to Chicago where the work paid better. Rented a heated garage and lived in it for two months, working during the day as often as I could get work. And experimenting on evenings and weekends. I finally realized I could never get away from the dust, so about six months ago I rented an apartment and just spent my free time at the garage. Meanwhile I went back to the library to study up on copyrights and trade-marks and found a patent attorney. And that brings me to today. Jane was nice enough to pretend to be an old friend and witness my signature."

Evaline beamed a dazzling smile at them, raised a fist, and said, "Whoopee!"

"Nice girl, isn't she?" Jane said as they started home.

"Hmm," Shelley said. "Pleasant. Not necessarily nice. I didn't like the idea of her making money writing other students' chemistry papers."

"No, I didn't either. But, Shelley, if we'd grown up without parents, without money, and wanted to get ahead in life, we might have chosen to do something not quite right."

"I don't think we would have."

Jane let it go. She thought back to her own child-hood, spent traveling around with her diplomat father and mother. She wasn't a good person to make such a judgment. She and her sister, Marty, had often been placed in boarding schools when it wasn't appropriate to take children along on her father's missions. Both of them had been rigidly trained to always be polite and gracious. It didn't stick with Marty, though, when she got to live her own life.

"Could we stop off just a moment at the project?" Shelley asked. "I forgot to measure the basement. And we haven't even seen the third floor where the gables are."

"Dormers," Jane automatically corrected her. "I guess so. I left dinner with instructions to put it all in the oven at five-thirty. And it's that time now. Won't be ready for at least half an hour."

Everyone had apparently left the job site. No trucks, no sign of lights left on, and plenty of parking space. "I brought along flashlights," Shelley said. "I have no idea if there are light fixtures down there."

The front door wasn't locked. "No wonder anyone can wander in here," Jane said. "Bitsy and Sandra should lock up everything when the workers are gone."

"That's just one of many things they aren't doing right," Shelley said, opening the basement door and feeling for a light switch along the wall. When she found one, an old-style push-button, light flooded the stairway.

"Oh my God!" Jane exclaimed. "There's a body down there!"

12

Shelley and Jane called their homes and let their children know they'd been delayed. "But turn the oven down to 225," Jane said to Todd.

"What's up, Mom?"

"There's been an accident at the place that's being renovated. I'll be home as soon as I can. I have to get off the phone now."

"Are you and Mrs. Nowack okay?"

"Perfectly okay. Don't worry," Jane said in the chirpiest voice she could manage, and it wasn't easy. Shelley had already dialed 911 from her cell phone, and they could hear sirens in the distance almost immediately.

"Shouldn't we go down there and see if we can help her?" Jane had asked.

"I don't think so," Shelley said, her voice shaking. "I'm very sure from the angle of her neck that she's dead. Let's just stay by the front door. I'm sorry I pushed that light button. I might have put a fingerprint over someone else's."

Two ambulances arrived at the same moment, and Shelley told them where to find the basement door. Mel VanDyne arrived only a moment later. And very angry to see them.

"I just finished all my work and got this call. What the hell are you two doing here?"

"Go check out the situation and we'll explain later," Jane said, understanding his frustration. They hadn't had any time together for over a week, and were both looking forward to his getting free for a while.

Shelley asked Jane, "Didn't Mel know what we were doing?"

Jane shook her head. "He's been frantically busy for the last week. Three different cases to wrap up. Mostly all we've been doing has been playing phone tag. No wonder he's mad at us. Now he's probably going to get stuck with this, just when he was expecting a bit of peace and quiet."

"But we'll be able to give him the background material and our impressions of the people working here. Won't he be the least grateful?"

Jane just rolled her eyes in disbelief that Shelley could say something that innocent with a straight face.

Mel was back shortly, thunder in his look. "I presume you know who the victim is?"

"Sandra Anderson," Jane said. "She is—or maybe was—the contractor."

"What does that mean, 'is or was'?"

"The last time I spoke with the owner," Shelley answered, "she was getting ready to fire Sandra."

"And who's the owner of this wreck, if you don't mind telling me?" Mel asked, still deeply in sarcastic mode.

"Bitsy Burnside," Jane said, pretending she didn't realize he was making a nasty remark. "If you can wait a sec, I think I have her telephone number in my purse." She rummaged while Mel fumed and found the crumpled deposit slip she'd written it on. She handed it over and asked, "May we go home now?"

"Please do. I remember where to find you," he said with a sigh.

"If you can get away, dinner's in the oven," Jane offered.

"Do you *really* think? Never mind." He turned away and disappeared.

Jane and Shelley fled. "Do you think she just tripped and fell, maybe?" Jane asked on the way home.

"I didn't see a purse. The police must not have found one either if Mel had to ask us her name. I never saw her without one. No, I don't think she tripped all by herself. Someone pushed her."

———

Bitsy called Jane later in the evening. "Jane, this is so awful! I'm afraid that detective thinks I killed Sandy. He said he'd spoken to you and Shelley, and I got the impression you knew him before."

"I'm dating him," Jane admitted.

"You're kidding! No, I guess you're not. Sandy and I did have a big blowup when I told her I'd hired the contractor I'd originally gotten a bid from. But I had no reason to harm her. Can't you explain that to your detective?"

"He's an intelligent man, Bitsy. This is what he successfully does for a living. He doesn't jump to conclusions. And he really wouldn't welcome my input."

There was a long silence on the line. Finally, sounding tearful, Bitsy croaked, "You don't think I could have done such a thing, do you?"

"No, of course not," Jane lied. If Bitsy had shoved Sandra down the steps, she certainly didn't want to act as if she suspected her for fear that she herself might become the next victim. "I'm just telling you he's an expert at what he does and he'll find out by himself what happened to Sandra." This wasn't precisely the truth. Jane and Shelley had contributed domestic insights to Mel on a couple of other cases. He called this dangerous snooping. They regarded it as helping.

Bitsy went on, not at all reassured, "But I left the

renovation before she did. The discussion was getting needlessly ugly and I thought there was nothing else productive to say, so I left the house, meaning to come back and lock up after everyone had gone. Surely someone saw me leaving, or knew I'd gone while she was still standing in the yard yelling at me as I drove off. I'm sure everybody was gawking and eavesdropping. Some of the workers really disliked her. But I was too upset by the confrontation to remember to go back and lock up when she was gone."

"Then everything should be okay," Jane said, "if you have witnesses."

"Half a dozen, at least. Everyone was upstairs still working and Sandy was screaming so loudly, I'm sure they heard it. Your detective did ask for everyone's names and addresses."

My detective, Jane thought. It made him sound like her personal bodyguard.

Jane immediately called Shelley. "Are you finished with dinner? I just got a hysterical call from Bitsy."

"I have to supervise some homework first. It'll be about a half-hour."

Jane's own supervision consisted of looking into Todd's bedroom door, where she could see the screen of his computer. He was obviously constructing grids for his prime number project. Katie was on the other phone line, giggling.

"Time to hang up and get your homework done," Jane said.

"I don't have any, and Jenny and I are making plans for next weekend," she said.

"Be sure to clear them with me," Jane warned as she went back downstairs to load the dishwasher.

Shelley was dead on time. "So what did Bitsy say to you?"

"That she thinks 'my detective' thinks she did it."

"Your detective? How did she know about you and Mel?"

"He must have mentioned speaking to us. Apparently she got the idea he already knew us. I admitted it. She wanted me to influence him."

"Fat chance!" Shelley exclaimed.

"She didn't understand when I explained that he always got the right perp," Jane said, pouring them each a cup of hot decaf coffee and setting a plate of grocery-store cookies on the kitchen table.

"She thought I meant I thought she'd done it," Jane finished up. "I told her I thought no such thing."

"Good for you. We don't want to make an enemy of her if she turns out to be guilty."

"She said there was a horrible blowup when she fired Sandra. Lots of yelling. She felt that all the workers heard and saw the part where Bitsy ran away in her car with Sandra screaming at her in the front yard. I suppose if that's true, she isn't the guilty party."

Shelley considered this. "Maybe not. Frankly, I can see how they both felt as if they were the injured party. Maybe Bitsy came back for one more round. Maybe she even came back to apologize. Either scenario could have led to a shoving match. It might have been an accident."

"At the top of the basement stairs with the door open?" Jane asked. "And her purse missing?"

"How do we know it's missing? Maybe it skittered away when she fell, or went under the stairs."

"I'm sure the police thought of that, Shelley."

"Hmm. I guess that is unlikely. What about Bitsy's ex-husband?"

"What about him?"

"He obviously had a high level of contempt for her. When he stopped by the house to harass her, it was obvious he knew a lot about what was going on. Maybe he intended to get her into even more trouble by causing a death."

"He seemed the nasty sort who might do so, but would he take such a risk? She was already in enough trouble she'd brought on herself," Jane said, adding, "Have another cookie, please. I'll eat all of them if you don't."

Shelley took an experimental nibble. "They're not bad. So, who else might be responsible? What about Evaline? She didn't like Sandra. She complained about being called 'Ev' as if it were for Everett."

"That's a trivial thing. Not worth killing for. What about the furnace guy? He was really very angry about having to get the rotten shrimp out of the ductwork. And I don't blame him. Such a horrible smell."

"I'd guess furnace guys are used to finding nasty things in ducts," Shelley replied. "Dead possums, squirrels, and such. And it's not as if Sandra weren't going to be hit up for a bigger bill, because it was her fault."

"Sandra wasn't paying the bills. Bitsy was, remember."

"We just keep coming back to Bitsy, don't we?" Shelley asked.

"Yes, we do. I wonder what they actually said to each other. What if Sandra was threatening to sue Bitsy if she were fired? That, on top of all the other expenses, might have put Bitsy over the edge. But there's a lot we don't know."

"Like what?"

"Who else disliked Sandra?" Jane asked. "She, too, has an ex-husband. At least I think so. Wasn't that supposed to be the reason she took her mother's maiden name back?"

"I thought that was so utterly silly, I put it out of my mind. I don't know if she did have a husband. But what about the other workers? Was someone else, besides Wesley the furnace guy, furious about her not keeping the site secure? Maybe valuable tools had been stolen?"

"That, again, would eventually become Bitsy's responsibility," Jane pointed out. "It was really up to her to make sure the doors were locked. She's the owner of the property. It's her insurance company that would have to pay for the tools if they were stolen or damaged."

"Back to Bitsy again. Do you really think she didn't do it herself?"

"I've never liked Bitsy much, but I just can't imagine her killing someone. Can you?"

"I really don't know her well enough to guess," Shelley admitted. "I guess we're going to have to let Mel figure it out. After all, it is his job."

"But we could help him out a little," Jane said. "The workers think of us as just other people who had to put up with both Bitsy and Sandra. They'd be more gossipy with us than with Mel."

13

The police department had closed the renovation house the next day to complete their physical search of the premises, which left Jane and Shelley free to catch up with real life. They each made heavy hits at the grocery store, paid and mailed bills, and did cleaning, and in the early afternoon, they joined back up to go to the library and check out a lot of expensive decorating books. Jane didn't hear from Mel and didn't try to call him when he was in such a bad mood.

They spent the afternoon poring over the books, gleaning many good ideas, especially for bathrooms and kitchens. Shelley had her copy of the measurements and took copious notes of what might fit where. Jane's notes were about styles and terms she was learning.

"This is the fun part," Jane said. "I'm feeling a little better about the possibility of actually doing this."

"It depends on a lot of things," Shelley reminded her. "What sort of contract Bitsy comes up with. And I'm sure she's not even thinking about it now. Not to mention what the police might be discovering. You don't want to just give Mel a call, do you?"

"I'm keeping a low profile until he's over his snit," Jane said. "It's not in my best interest to irritate him further when he's been so overworked."

"I'd sure like to know what he's learned about the other people involved," Shelley said. "And I wonder who this new contractor is. Apparently it's a man. I wonder what he's going to think about all the women workers."

"You don't suppose he'll replace them, do you?"

"I wouldn't think he could. Most of them are probably under contract to Bitsy."

"But if the contracts were really with Sandra . . . ?"

"Oh, dear. I hadn't thought of that. Our contract, though obviously devised by Sandra, was supposed to be with Bitsy. I'd assume the others were as well."

"Then he's stuck with the workers unless they bail out voluntarily."

"Some of them may," Shelley said. "But most of them seemed to be quite good at what they were doing."

"It's a shame we don't know more about most of them," Jane said. "After getting to know a bit about

Evaline, it makes me wonder how and why the others, like Jack and Henry, happened to get into what are traditionally men's jobs. And seem to be quite good at them. I bet they won't bail out. The work they're doing on the house will be a fine credit for them to get other jobs."

"You're probably right. Maybe we need to get to know them better when the work can go on," Shelley agreed.

"But not in front of Mel," Jane warned. "We'll have to see them away from work if the house is still crawling with police."

"Didn't we get a list of them?"

"I didn't," Jane said.

"I'm running home for my file. I'm sure in the wad of paperwork Bitsy gave me, there's a list of the workers."

"Why would she give either of us that information?"

"For consultation purposes, I suppose. To see what they think about the feasibility of what we're shopping for. Like the wiring for the kitchen, say, or the necessary plumbing and dimensions of the bathrooms. I'm going to run home and see if I'm right about that list. I'm sure I didn't imagine it. I just wasn't especially interested when I spotted it."

"We haven't met or heard about the plumber yet, have we?"

Shelley was back in a few minutes. "I was right. Here are the names and telephone numbers. But no plumber mentioned. What would you say to getting together somewhere tomorrow, if the house is still closed, with Jacqueline and Henrietta?"

"On what excuse?"

"We can say we need to know what the plans are for the finished woodwork so we don't clash with it on the furniture," Shelley said.

"And then just chat with them about generalities? I like it."

Shelley made the call and set up a time and place for lunch the next day.

"You two are experts at your work and we don't want to do anything that compromises it," Shelley said when they met with the two women.

It was interesting to see the pair in their street clothes rather than their work clothes. Jack was in a pink sundress with a pretty lacy collar and a touch of very feminine makeup. She was truly a Jacqueline when she wasn't working. Henry was wearing a gender-neutral suit in dark blue with trousers, with a very elegant blue-and-white-striped blouse. There was a pretty enamel pin on her lapel.

They were both so nicely dressed that they put Jane and Shelley in the shade. Both of them were in nice-enough slacks, blouses, and lightweight sweaters because restaurants tended to turn the air conditioning way up until the late fall. Of one silent accord, they called their two guests by their full real names.

Shelley pulled out some sample paint chips, and while the waitress cooled her heels waiting for them to get to the menus, Shelley asked Jacqueline's and Henrietta's advice on colors for the main area of the room they were currently working on. All very professional and proper for strangers who were expected to work together.

Jane was particularly taken with Jacqueline's alternative suggestions for colors.

"Something a little warmer, I think," Jacqueline said. "The blues might be lighter and more subdued. And if it were up to me, the cream might be just a bit more golden."

Shelley pulled out yet more paint chips from her notebook. "Like these?" she asked. "I think you're right."

Jane nudged Shelley. "The waitress is waiting. We ought to order before she becomes more annoyed. It's crowded, and she wants to get us moving along."

"I think we've sorted it out satisfactorily," Shelley said graciously, putting little marks on the back of the paint samples and stowing them away. "We're really grateful for your ideas."

They all studied their menus out and ordered salads, except for Henrietta, who ordered a burger, cooked medium rare, with fries.

Then the real purpose of the meeting arose.

"How did both of you choose to do such unusual jobs?" Jane asked.

Jacqueline and Henrietta smiled at each other. Jacqueline said, "You can't imagine how often we're asked this. We both grew up with fathers who were carpenters and naturally developed an interest. I decided to go to trade school instead of college, and Henrietta did so as well. We met at the trade school."

"I was a year ahead of Jacqueline," Henrietta put in, "and already doing several small jobs the trade school set up for me. Furniture, mainly. Little Mission–style tables and chairs. Since we were the only women there except one of the teachers, we naturally got to know each other. I asked Jacqueline to help me with the finishing work. I have a talent for design, but Jackie has the eye for color."

"We've worked together ever since," Jacqueline said with a smile. "But this is the biggest job we've gotten so far. It's really challenging, and Bitsy's giving us free rein to use our skills."

"It's just such a shame that poor Bitsy hooked herself up with Sandra," Henrietta said glumly. "She really wasn't qualified for the job. She had an entirely different agenda."

"What was that?"

"Oh, I thought you'd have noticed," Henrietta said. "The big-deal feminist thing. We both fell in with that when we got out into the real world together, but recovered from it quite soon. It's pointless. Once you've done a couple of jobs well, you get recommended to other people by the quality of your work, not your gender."

"Don't you have trouble mostly with male contractors?" Shelley said.

"We normally work for individual customers. And we still do custom furniture," Jacqueline said. "When the few contractors we've worked with see our portfolios of work we've done, we usually get the job."

"Except for that one really macho guy who was terrified to bits about lesbians," Henrietta said. "He seemed to think it was a disease of some sort."

"That's odd," Shelley said. "It seems as if most macho types are more scared of male gays. More of a threat to them, they seem to think."

"That's usually true in our experience as well," Henrietta said. "But Sandra took her militant feminism far too seriously. I'm sorry she died and all that, but it was divisive. Calling us all by men's names was so stupid and insulting. Nobody's ever done that to us before. I refused to address her as Sandy. I think Bitsy's the only one who does so."

"You really didn't like working with her?"

"The name thing was silly," Jacqueline said. "I don't mind being called Jackie. It's a common nickname and easier than Jacqueline to say. But what I really disliked was that she wasn't a knowledgeable contractor. The contracts that Bitsy let her draw up were ridiculous and showed her ignorance of the business."

"We found that to be true as well," Shelley said. "We still aren't really hired, you know, until the contract we were offered is extensively amended."

"Don't worry about it," Henrietta said. "Bitsy speaks well of your tastes. She'll go along with what you want, I'd guess. She's known you both for a long time, hasn't she?"

"Yes," Shelley said. "We go back years to PTA work."

That made everyone laugh.

When their food arrived, they fell to eating, and conversation was solely about the food. As they were considering dessert, Jane asked, "Did anyone truly hate Sandra?"

"Hate? I wouldn't go that far," Jacqueline said. "She was seriously annoying and not very good at what she was trying to do. I think the only person who genuinely disliked her was Thomasina."

"We haven't met Thomasina yet," Jane said. "She's the electrician, isn't she?"

"And she's very good," Henrietta said. "But she had her toolbox stolen and went haywire because Sandra was responsible for making sure any tools that couldn't be hauled home every night were securely locked up. And there was that time Jackie got a serious shock when she turned the planer on."

Jacqueline objected. "It was nothing. Just a jolt that knocked me off my feet."

"It knocked you out, Jackie! Don't be shy about it," Henrietta said. "You were lucky it didn't kill you."

"I'm fine. And I'm sure it wasn't anything Thomasina did wrong. The planer worked fine the day before and she was off sick the day before that. It was just another of those nasty tricks someone was playing. And I wasn't knocked out by the shock. It was because I jumped back, tripped, and hit my head on one of the sawhorses."

Jane and Shelley looked at each other with alarm.

"We hadn't heard about this," Jane said, any thoughts she'd had about dessert completely forgotten.

14

Thomasina is the one we need to meet next," Shelley said as they were on their way home.

"She sounds like a good suspect, doesn't she?"

"She may not have been the angriest one. We still don't know several of the others," Shelley reminded Jane.

"Who are we missing?"

Shelley consulted her sheet of workers. "There's Carl Stringfield, the guy who works with Evaline. The big tall man we watched casually twirl a big piece of Sheetrock slap up against the wall and place it perfectly. And, of course, the elusive plumber."

"I wonder how much of what we already know Mel knows."

After Shelley had sorted out this obscure sentence structure, she said, "We probably know more about their personalities and backgrounds. At least that's true of Bitsy, Evaline, Jacqueline, and Henrietta. But he's much more likely to be up to speed on the actual evidence of whether or not Sandra's death was a murder or a clumsy accident."

"I'll try to snag Mel tonight for dinner," Jane offered. "After all, he's only working one case now instead of three. He's going to feel strongly motivated to have a bit of a real life off the job."

"What are you going to make for dinner?" Shelley asked, getting to the heart of the plan. "What's his favorite dinner?"

"Steaks cooked medium rare on the grill. Twice-baked potatoes. Greasy, overcooked green beans. And he'll even pick at a salad if he's forced to."

"Then I'd leave out the salad," Shelley said with a grin. "I wonder what his terribly high-maintenance mother who's probably eaten at the most expensive restaurants in the country thinks of his tastes."

Jane shuddered at the thought of Mel's mother. She'd once spent a Christmas with Mel and ended up at Jane's, who found her formidable and clearly hostile to the idea of her son forming a romantic attachment to a woman she hadn't handpicked for him. Especially a widow with three children.

Jane had prevailed earlier and driven the two of them to lunch in her disreputable station wagon, so she just had to drop Shelley off and hit the grocery store after leaving a voice mail message on Mel's cell phone that he was invited to his favorite dinner. If that didn't get his full attention, nothing would.

When she returned, loaded down with groceries, there was a light flashing on the answering machine. "I wouldn't miss it for the world," Mel said. "Six-thirty?"

"We still don't know what happened to her," he said when they'd finished what he said was a fabulous meal. They'd eaten in the kitchen with Katie and Todd, but had gone outside to sit under the patio table umbrella for a glass of wine for dessert for Jane, a beer for Mel, who'd mellowed considerably since she'd last spoken with him.

"There's no clear sign of her being pushed down the stairs, but it wouldn't take an enormous force that would leave bruises," he said taking a sip of his beer. "This is good."

"Are you going to continue investigating?"

"We have to. The missing purse is one reason. Apparently nobody working at the site ever once saw Sandra without it. A bag with a long strap hung over her opposite shoulder so it couldn't be dropped or stolen."

"Even I noticed that. The first time we met her, Shelley and I stashed our purses between us. When I asked if Sandra wanted to put hers there as well, she acted like I'd spit in her glass."

"I sort of wish you had. That would have kept you out of this," Mel said with a laugh.

"And no sign of it in the house somewhere?"

"Nope. But the primary reason to treat it as a crime is that she was so heartily disliked by everyone on the project. Nobody has anything good to say about her. They're all very frank about it. She seems to have gone out of her way to offend people working on the house. Maybe one of them had a stronger motive than the criticism of her that they've voiced."

"Do you know yet when she died?"

"When she hit the basement floor," Mel said.

"I know that. I mean what time?"

"The pathologist says some time between three-thirty and five-thirty. Too bad she wasn't wearing a watch that stopped conveniently."

"That's quite a window of time," Jane said. "I suppose you've asked everyone working there if anyone disappeared for a while."

"Of course I did," Mel said, surprisingly mildly. "Everybody was doing his or her own job and didn't pay much attention to what the others were doing. Some said they went outside on their breaks for a cigarette, a couple took bathroom breaks. You can't break alibis like that."

There was a long companionable silence as they watched Max and Meow, Jane's cats, returning from the field behind her house after a long day of hunting mice and chipmunks. Mel rose to let them in the house, but Jane said, "No, please don't open that door. I want them to throw up the remains outside instead of on my floors."

It was another full five minutes before Jane admitted that she and Shelley had taken Jacqueline and Henrietta to lunch earlier.

Mel started to object, but Jane cut him off. "We had a legitimate reason to meet with them. We're supposed to be doing the decorating and they're the carpenters who are using all the special wood. We wanted to make sure the color scheme we had in mind for the first part of the house to be finished met their approval."

Mel yelped with laughter. "I'll bet you cleared up that part of your talk pretty quickly and plunged into pure gossip."

Jane smiled. "Of course we did. Were you told about Jacqueline's getting shocked and passing out?"

"The electrician told us all about it. The wiring had been tampered with. Not badly enough to kill her because when she plugged in whatever it was, the fuse blew. Or so the electrician says. And so does my assistant, who understands electricity. She passed out because she jumped backward, tripped, and struck her head on a sawhorse when she fell."

"The electrician is Thomasina, right? We haven't run across her yet."

"You're not going to enjoy it when you do. She's a really tough, foulmouthed woman who won't listen to what anyone else is asking or saying."

"Your prime suspect?"

"Not necessarily. But if any of them are truly mean enough to kill someone and I had choose at random, I'd like to pick her." He downed a little more of his glass of beer before continuing. He seemed to need it.

"She went on and on about the house never being locked up," he said, glowering at the memory of his interview with her. "Or even sufficiently boarding up the downstairs windows. I got the full rundown on what valuable tools were in her toolbox that had been stolen. By the time she got to the fact that her precious wiring had been tampered with, I feared she was going to have a stroke right on the spot. Like most self-employed people, she's underinsured, and if Jacqueline had wanted to sue her for the accident, it could have gotten really ugly."

"I think we'll keep our distance from her in that case," Jane said with a smile.

A cat threw up outside.

"Excuse me for a moment," she said as she went into the garage to get a shovel to heave the remains over the back fence.

Mel was laughing out loud when she returned from this common errand. "I've never known a woman so calm about pieces of dead animals."

Jane looked surprised. "I do this a couple times a week. Most of the time inside the house. Aren't you glad you don't live here? All my kids have learned how to imitate the nasty sounds that precede a cat upchucking and sometimes do it in the middle of the night to make me think I don't dare get out of bed without turning on a light. Didn't I tell you about the time I nearly took a header in the bathroom on a mouse's head? Just like stepping on a marble, albeit a fuzzy one."

Mel laughed but then turned serious. "You're a remarkable woman."

"No, I'm an ordinary woman with two cats," she said, leaning forward to kiss him. "You must have just grown up without cats."

"Without dogs, too," he said, being a bit pathetic.

"Don't start with me about dogs! Training Willard took longer than potty-training a male child."

He chuckled and said, "Want to go for a little drive?"

"To your apartment?" Jane asked with a gleam in her eye.

"We could drop in there. After all, I need to thank you again for dinner."

When she got home later, she saw that Shelley's kitchen light was still on. The phone was already ringing when Jane came in the door.

"What did Mel tell you?" Shelley asked.

"I don't remember," Jane said dreamily.

"You were at his apartment tonight, weren't you?

15

Early the next morning Jane took the cats and Willard out in the yard and sat contentedly watching them while she had her first cup of coffee and one of the three cigarettes she allowed herself per day. She wished she could quit entirely, and often forgot to smoke one of them. In bad winters, she seldom braved the weather outside to smoke more than one, but three a day was better than twenty.

When she went back inside, the answering machine had a message from her sister, Marty. She sighed. Marty called her only when she couldn't remember where in the world their parents were, and it was always for financial help. So she'd call Jane, and after listening to silly pleas that fell on Jane's deaf ears,

Jane would give her the current telephone number for their parents. One time Marty asked if she could use Jane's calling card account, to which Jane replied that she most certainly could not.

Why didn't Marty break down and buy a computer? She'd married or lived off a string of wealthy men. That way she could always reach anyone she wanted by E-mail. Jane and her parents were in touch at least weekly, often daily, and it was free, unlike phone calls to foreign countries.

As usual, Jane didn't return the call right away. Sometimes she got lucky if she dawdled and whatever problem Marty imagined had already solved itself. And on occasion, Marty herself couldn't even remember. This evening would be soon enough.

The phone rang while she was writing down the number on the caller ID. She wondered vaguely where Marty was now. She didn't recognize the area code.

She saw that it was Shelley and picked up.

"Are you back to real life yet? I saw you sitting outside grinning. Nice evening with Mel?"

"Unfortunately, I am back to the nitty-gritty. Come on over and I'll feed you some kind of breakfast."

Shelley was there in about half a minute. "Isn't it great when all the kids want for breakfast is an egg sandwich and a bottle of orange juice to eat and drink on their way to school?" she said. "I shudder at the recollection of having to cook pancakes or bacon at the crack of dawn."

"All I have is some sort of healthy granola bars," Jane said apologetically. "But they're not bad. Here you go," she said, tossing a couple on the kitchen table and pouring their coffee. "Got a call from my sister while I was outside."

"What does she need now?"

"I haven't called back to see. Remember the time she wanted me to rush to Seattle because she had to have an ingrown toenail removed and expected the whole family to gather around to comfort her?"

"I'd forgotten that one. The one I liked best was the time you were supposed to go to Nashville—or was it Savannah?—to help her pick out a dress for a banquet."

"Savannah, I think. I suspect she thought I'd pay for the dress, and naturally pay for my plane fare as well. The worst ones are when she's getting divorced, and her money's tied up in court, and she wants huge loans. I can always say the kids have some sort of program at school and I can't go anywhere when she wants me to fly halfway across the country, but it's harder to turn her down on money."

"I think that would be easier. Just tell her you don't have any."

"She knows better than to believe that. Even my parents won't do it. I don't know why she continues to ask them."

"Never?"

"Not unless she has a really good story. Then they

wire her a couple hundred dollars and do the same for me."

Shelley reached for a second fruit-and-granola bar. "These aren't as bad as I expected. I want to talk to you about Thomasina. But do you want to call your sister back first?"

"Neither of those options would be my first choice. I think I'd rather have a week in Bermuda. Sprawled on a beach with a good book, thinking about my sins."

"Then let's talk about Thomasina first. I know what Mel said about her, how tough and nasty she is. But he's a cop and lots of people don't like talking to cops."

"You have a point there," Jane admitted. "Especially when they fear they're being investigated as a possible suspect."

"But you and I aren't cops. We'll just chat with her about some innocuous subject such as how many electrical outlets she plans for those rooms they're working on now. Pretend we're thinking about furniture and lamp placement. And then ease with enormous sympathy into what went wrong with the wiring."

"And also pretend to understand?"

"Of course."

"Since you think this sounds sensible, I think I'll play the role of the nodding sidekick, if you don't mind. I don't even *want* to understand wiring."

"That's okay by me. Let's go over to the House of Seven Mabels and see if she's around."

Jane didn't understand why this pun tickled Shelley so much. Shelley usually didn't even understand puns.

"And that Mel isn't there," Jane said. "That's understood, isn't it?"

"Did Mel happen to mention whether the house is open to us yet when you were with him last night?"

"Are you insane?" Jane said, hoping she wasn't blushing. "We didn't talk about that at all."

"Guess we're going to have to go over there, then," Shelley said with an expression that on a less refined woman would have been called a smirk.

They took a few minutes to put on their jeans and boots so they'd fit in with the workers. Shelley was getting used to being seen in public in jeans, as long as they were freshly pressed. They were greeted at the locked front door by Bitsy, who looked as if she hadn't slept for a couple of days. "I want you two to meet Joe Budley. He's now our contractor."

She led them to the old dining room, where new, sturdy plywood was being installed by a group of men they'd never seen. Strong young men, most of whom sported goatees, which Jane thought was one of the most unattractive facial attributes a man could choose deliberately.

Bitsy introduced them to Joe Budley, who was an enormous, burly-looking man with violently red hair and matching eyebrows that nearly met in the middle of his face. He, too, wore jeans, boots, and a plaid shirt, but had on a sport coat as well that strained at the armholes and across his burly shoulders.

He shook their hands with a paralyzing grip and said, in an accent straight from Oklahoma, "Glad tuh meetcha, ladies."

"Jane and Shelley are our decorators. Or they will be when I can get around to preparing their contract for their agreement."

"Women are good at that," he said. This was apparently a dismissal of women being good at other things, or so it seemed to Jane. Then she realized, to her horror, that she was thinking like Sandra. That any man who spoke about women was automatically deriding them. Immediately upon the thought, Joe blew her theory.

"Well, you girls get along with what you were doing while Bitsy here and I talk over things."

Shelley looked around with apparent surprise. "What girls are you talking to? I don't see girls here. I didn't bring my daughter along, and neither did Mrs. Jeffry. Do you, by some freak chance, consider all the talented workers on the job to be girls?"

Joe said, "You're one of them, aren't you?"

"One of what?" Shelley asked innocently.

"One of them feminists."

"Not until today," Shelley said. "Only my own father is entitled to think of me as a girl."

"I'm right sorry to hear that," he groused, turning

his back to her and engaging Bitsy in a discussion of replacement workers.

Bitsy, perhaps inspired by Shelley, maybe just coming into her own, or simply having been driven mad by lack of rest, asked, "Why should we do that, Joey *boy*? Do you find their work unsatisfactory without even looking at it? I've hired professionals in their fields. Some of them are women. But if you don't want to be the contractor for this, so be it."

Jane and Shelley exchanged a quick glance. Bitsy was really going out on a limb. Contractors who were ready to step in at the drop of a hat weren't thick on the ground, not even in Chicago. The good ones were all busy with other jobs.

Astonishingly, Joe made an effort to apologize without actually saying the word "sorry." "Well, if you—women—feel this way, we ought to get on with looking over what you've done so far. And make up a work schedule to get it completed."

"Very well," Bitsy said glacially.

Bitsy and Joe ascended the stairs, Joe letting her go first. Whether out of courtesy or just to see her from behind no one ever knew. Shelley was still so angry she was red in the face. Jane had never seen her this way. "Calm down. He's just an old fart."

"Girls! GIRLS!" Shelley exclaimed.

"Good thing nobody has a blood pressure cuff handy to slap on you," Jane said. "Shelley, let's just walk out of here and never come back."

Shelley stomped outside ahead of Jane, but instead of going to the car, she sat down on the front steps. "If I'd lived a hundred years ago, I'd need to have a nice lie-down with a cold cloth over my eyes."

"It's not a bad idea today," Jane said, trying to urge Shelley back onto her feet.

Shelley was back to her normal coloring, and her expression turned serene. "No, we can't run away. It would look like a flounce. Exactly what the jerk expects of women. I hate to admit this, but Bitsy did a better job on him than I did."

Jane's mouth dropped open. She'd never heard Shelley admit this about anyone before.

16

The police still had most of the ground floor roped off but had allowed the workers to go upstairs to continue their work. Fortunately, the investigators were just tech people, packing up their gear to leave. No sign of Mel.

When Jane and Shelley got upstairs, Henrietta and Jacqueline greeted them and Evaline said in a muffled voice through her face mask, "Hi there, you two." She was busy using her sander on some of the Sheetrock joints. It had a small vacuum bag and created almost no dust, but she must have simply been in the habit of wearing the mask to sand, whether she needed it or not.

Wesley, the furnace guy, came up, welded one last piece of ductwork, and said, "As far as I'm concerned,

I'm done in here. All I have to do now is turn the furnace on to make sure it's up and running again. Go ahead and Sheetrock the ceiling if Thomasina's ready."

"Not quite. Another hour for the ceiling fixtures," a voice boomed behind Jane.

Jane turned and saw a gigantic woman with big hands and big blond hair that looked as if she'd suffered a real electrical shock, though the hair was probably just overbleached and overpermed.

"You must be Thomasina," Shelley said. "Or do you prefer Tom?"

"Thomasina, if you don't mind. Nobody but that idiot contractor ever called me Tom. And you are . . . ?"

They introduced themselves, and she enveloped both their hands in turn in her huge paw. "Welcome aboard. I saw Joe Budley on my way up. Is he Bitsy's new contractor?"

"I think so," Jane said. "Do you know him?"

"Worked for him once 'bout five years ago. Not crazy about the guy, but he does move things along pretty briskly," Thomasina said. "Sometimes too briskly."

"We'll need to consult with you later, if you have a bit of free time," Shelley said.

"Why?"

"About placement of the wall sockets and ceiling lighting."

"As for the walls, I always put at least two sockets on each. Three, sometimes even four, if it's a long wall.

It's overkill, but in these days of computers and all sorts of gadgets that need juice, it can't hurt to have extras. I'll have some time to jaw with you over the ceiling lighting over lunch if you want."

"That would be fine," Shelley said.

So much for Thomasina being the horror that Mel described. Though rather stunningly unattractive, she was very pleasant—so far, Jane thought. But still, she hoped they didn't have to clash over ceiling lighting. That might bring out the belligerent woman Mel knew.

Bitsy and Joe were huddled over a piece of plywood on sawhorses, looking over the plans, which were being kept from rolling up with various blocks of scrap wood and hammers. Joe kept looking around to see how far the work had progressed. If he found fault with any of it, he had the common sense to keep it to himself in front of the workers.

"Are those Sandra's plans?" Shelley asked, strolling over to look. "Bitsy and I have discussed the fact that the measurements aren't entirely correct."

Jane suddenly had an insight that had nothing to do with this job. She'd been creeping through what she hoped would turn into a historical novel for a couple of years. She realized as Shelley spoke that the spooky house where the main character lived was almost a character itself, and that one of the problems she'd always faced with the writing was that she could picture the sprawling old house sitting on a hostile crag. But she had no idea what it was like inside. Her character had looked out over the dark, cold sea from her bedroom window. That was all she knew.

Jane desperately wanted to run and get a computer program that would allow her to make the house plans so that when her heroine walked from the bedroom suite to the stairs, Jane could actually picture how many steps it would take and what other doorways were in the upper hall. And she had a new computer it would work on. The plans Shelley, Joe, and Bitsy were looking at had to have been computer-generated.

Thomasina was back at work. Shelley had presented her own measurements to Joe Budley, and Jane pulled Shelley aside and quietly said, "Do you really need me to talk to Thomasina? I have something I really want to do with my book today."

Shelley looked pleased. "I haven't heard you mention your book forever. I'm glad to hear you're still working on it. Go ahead. I can handle this myself."

Jane rushed to her car, headed for the nearest computer center, and dashed home with the program the clerk had recommended. Not a truly professional one. Those, she learned, cost thousands of dollars and you had to take classes to learn how they worked. But lots of do-it-yourselfers used the one she had bought for a hundred dollars. She dithered a bit reading the instructions for installing the program and was astonished when she got it right on the first try.

She didn't have any car pool duty today and realized when Katie and Todd barged through the kitchen door, slamming their backpacks on the kitchen table, that what had seemed like mere minutes had been at least five hours of concentrated creativity. It wasn't writing, of course, but she had the basics of the house in her mind, and when she finished the last details, she'd be eager to get back to work on the endless book. Maybe it wouldn't truly be endless. It was odd to feel both exhausted and exhilarated at the same time.

"Kids, come look at this!" she shouted down the stairs.

Katie looked at the screen. "What's that?"

"Where Priscilla lives," Jane said.

"Who's Priscilla?" Todd asked, leaning closer.

"The woman in the book I've been working on for as long as I can remember."

"I don't see any bathrooms," Todd said.

"Oh!" Jane said, putting the palm of her hand on her forehead.

"But it's sure a cool program," Todd said, glancing through the instruction manual.

"I have you to thank," Jane said. "If I hadn't bought this computer, I wouldn't have ever been able to do this. The old one couldn't have coped with something this elaborate. Would you have a little time to help me figure out where to put the bathrooms?"

"After dinner. Sure."

"Dinner?" Jane asked as if she'd never heard the word. "What kind of carryout would you like?"

"Pizza!" both kids chorused.

"Then spring for delivery. Todd, you can help me while we wait."

When Shelley dropped in for coffee around eight o'clock, Katie said, "Mom's on the computer. You'll have to crowbar her hand off the mouse."

"What's she doing?"

"Making a house for Priscilla," Katie said with a laugh. "Go on upstairs. You'll probably have to beat her on the head to get her attention."

Katie was nearly right. Shelley had to call Jane's name three times before she noticed. "Shelley, this is so cool. Look at this."

Jane explained that when she saw Shelley, Bitsy, and Joe looking over the house plans, she'd realized they were done on a computer. She went on, showing Shelley every detail of the bleak, windswept house she was constructing.

Shelley had often nagged Jane, though gently, to finish the book and was truly delighted that this had inspired her to get back to it.

"I haven't seen you this excited about your book before. I think it's wonderful. But isn't it set in the 1800s? I think this kitchen you have on the ground floor would have been in the basement, or even a separate building if it was in the South. All the cooking was done with real wood fires and they didn't want them smoking up the whole house. That's the whole reason those domelike silver things were made to put over plates. So you carry the food quite a long way without it getting cold before it got to the dining room."

"Another head slapper," Jane said. "You're right."

"Doesn't this make you more interested in the house plans?"

Jane instantly felt a twinge of guilt. "Shelley, I'm sorry. I've been so obsessed with what I was doing that I didn't even ask how your meeting with Thomasina went."

"Pretty well. She explained to me at great length how someone gave Jacqueline a bit of a shock."

"And you understood?"

"Not in the least, but I pretended I did. I'm not sure she believed me. No, I *know* she didn't believe me, but it led to an interesting discussion. Thomasina said the liability insurance for electricians is right up there with malpractice policies for physicians. Hefty payments. And even more hefty penalties if a suit is brought against the electrician. She's so grateful that Jacqueline wasn't hurt seriously that she offered to pay the hospital bill. But she was really furious about Sandra allowing the house to be free to trespassers."

"She thought it was someone coming in off the street?"

"No. Thomasina suspects Joe Budley."

"Why?"

"She says word has gotten around in the trades that he has some troubles of his own with other projects and is involved in a couple of lawsuits over shoddy work, because he cuts corners to get projects done as fast as possible."

Jane saved her house plan and shut down the computer. As they went down the stairs to the kitchen, she asked, "You mean he could have been responsible for all the bad things so Sandra would be fired and Bitsy would have to take him on?"

"Remember, Bitsy had consulted him before she ran into Sandra. He lost a big job to a woman who wasn't even competent. Thomasina's pretty convinced he's behind the shrimp episode."

"Are you convinced?" Jane asked.

"Nope. I'd say it's Bitsy's ex-husband, if I had to guess. Or someone who had a personal grudge against Sandra."

Jane said, "That might be anyone who was forced to work with or for her."

Shelley nodded. "Exactly."

17

Jane was wide-awake at six in the morning, eager to get back to Priscilla's house plans. Todd's bedroom light was on as well. "How's it going?" she said, stepping into his room.

"I have a lot to do before I can even start the real work," he said. "See, I figure I've got to have at least ten thousand numbers to see a pattern."

"That many?"

"At least. First I'm making a regular grid. Fifty wide. With five digits in each cell. Making the grid is easy. Cut and paste, but filling in the numbers is going to take a long time."

Jane looked at the grid. The number for one was really four zeros and the one at the end. It was red.

"Reds are prime numbers?"

"Right. I just keep putting numbers in and when I get bored with entering them, I go back, multiply by twos, and make them black."

"There's a nine thing I learned when I had a summer job at a bank," Jane said. "Any number like . . ." She punched in multiplication in the little adding machine beside him. Nine times eighty-three. It came up seven hundred forty-seven.

"See? The two sevens equal fourteen and with the four they equal eighteen, which is divisible by nine. It's always that way."

"Cool! How'd you know that?"

"My dinky job at a bank one summer during high school was checking tapes of wads of checks. They were always added twice. When they didn't add up exactly, this wise old woman, who'd started at the bank doing the same boring job when she was my age, told me that if the difference in the two tapes equaled something divisible by nine, at least one number on a tape had been transposed."

"Transposed?"

"Yes, like sixty-three for thirty-six. It made it easier to find the error. So I played around with nines and discovered how neat they are. You want to shower first?"

"Okay. I'll leave you some hot water."

Todd saved his grid, shut down his computer, and

headed for the kids' bathroom before Katie could pull herself together and occupy it for half an hour.

Jane went downstairs, made peanut-butter-and-jelly sandwiches, and got out little plastic containers of orange juice for Todd's and Katie's traveling-to-school breakfasts. Then she hotfooted it back upstairs to work on her house plans. Two hours later, she realized that the house was quiet except for Willard barking at the back door to be let out.

It had seemed mere minutes since she'd sat down at the computer. *This could be dangerous,* she thought. *Time just flies away when I'm doing this.*

When she opened the back door, the cats shot out between Willard's legs and headed for the field. He snapped at them and growled but made no real effort to make contact. They had sharp claws and he didn't. Jane fixed a cup of coffee and went outside as well. She looked around the yard at her fledgling gardens and realized it was going to be an awfully nice day to do a bit of weeding and deadheading.

"You're not moving very fast this morning, are you?" Shelley asked as she came through the gate. "Sleep hair, still in your robe."

"I've been up for hours, though," Jane said. "I've been playing with the computer. I've realized that since Priscilla's house is on a steep hill, there have to be lots of steps going up and down to rooms at different levels."

"Aren't you making this even harder for yourself?"

"Yes, but that's part of the fun. Do we have anything at the renovation we have to do today? I thought I might tidy up the yard if not."

"I don't think so. Bitsy called a few minutes ago. She's working with her attorney on our contract today."

"Good for her. I half hope it's not as good as we'll like."

"That's because, like your son, you have found another obsession," Shelley said, taking a seat at the picnic table with her own cup of steaming coffee. "But keep in mind, even if the contract is okay, this isn't a full-time job. And it involves a lot of shopping."

"There is that to consider. Not to mention making a bit of extra money."

"Quite a bit," Shelley said, "if we get our way. I think you're right about it being a good day to garden."

"I had a bit of a coup and impressed Todd this morning," Jane said, smiling. She told Shelley about the nines tricks.

"That can't be right all the time," Shelley said.

"Try it and see," Jane said smugly, standing up and yawning. "I need to shower. Want to lunch somewhere?"

"Of course."

Jane had never seriously gardened until the previous spring. She and Shelley had taken a course about it and

imported fake gardens for the garden tour near the end
of the class. But it had really inspired both of them.

What she liked best about it was pulling weeds. It
was therapeutic to tidy up nature. It was a relaxing solitary thing that had nothing to do with words or other
people. The best part was that it didn't take much
intelligence and allowed her mind to wander all over
the place.

While she was pulling out the crabgrass that in-
fested one part of her yard, she thought about her
imaginary house plans and how she could refine them.
As she worked on deadheading the coneflowers, she
considered Todd's project. While she loaded up the
trash with unwanted greenery and dead stuff, she
thought about the restoration of Bitsy's house.

It had seemed a curse to her from the beginning.
She'd wished all along that Shelley had never mentioned it. But things might be looking up. Just getting
a new contractor, no matter how obnoxious, who
locked up the place was a good thing. And if Shelley
could get a good enough contract out of Bitsy, it would
be a nice extra income just from shopping—something
that was fun to do with Shelley.

And since Sandra was gone, the feminist overtones
that had irritated nearly everyone had died down.

She went inside, tidied herself up, and took a glass
of iced tea outside to sit at the patio table and consider
how much nicer the yard looked. Mind still wandering,

she came back to Sandra. Mel hadn't told her anything more about the investigation. She wondered if, in the end, it would be considered an accident.

The missing purse, however, seemed to belie that. Even Jane, who didn't pay as much attention to habits like that, had noticed that Sandra was never without it. Maybe she had simply uncharacteristically set it down for a moment somewhere and it went out to the Dumpster with other debris. She wondered if the police at the scene of the crime had emptied the Dumpster searching for it.

Still, it was odd that Sandra had even gone anywhere near the basement. It would be hard to negotiate the steps in high heels, which she had been wearing that day. The steps were steep and narrow, and the light wasn't good. Jane tried to remember if there had been handrails and didn't think there were, but when Shelley had turned on the light and they saw the body, she hadn't studied much else.

If it wasn't an accident, someone had pushed her.

Probably someone working in the house. Or maybe not. But it would be risky for an outsider to come in without being noticed, when people were up and down the stairs, in and out of all the rooms, all the time. And if there was such a person, it was unlikely that he or she would just happen to come across Sandra alone at the head of the basement steps with the door open. If it was deliberate, it seemed more likely to be one of the workers rather than Bitsy's nasty ex-husband, or the new contractor snooping around a job he had wanted and wasn't hired for.

Shelley, looking as if she'd never gotten her fingernails dirty in her whole life, came through the gate to the backyard as Jane was pondering.

"It looks better," she said, looking around Jane's backyard. "And you look a lot better, too. I want you to see my backyard after lunch. I'm starving."

They went to their favorite Italian restaurant and sat in a secluded booth. They were rather late to lunch and were almost the last customers to come in.

"I was brooding over Sandra's death while I weeded," Jane said. "Do you know if they went through the Dumpster in case she'd put her purse down somewhere for once?"

"I have no idea. I assume they did," Shelley said. "It would be a good place to dispose of anything you didn't want to ever be seen again."

"Not necessarily," Jane said. "Uncle Jim took a load of stuff in a rented trailer to the city dump once and invited me to go along."

"And you went? Of your own free will?" Shelley hooted.

"It was interesting. Of course, the smell was horrible, but there was this vast hole in the ground with a lot of enormous earthmoving equipment shoving the garbage over the ledge. A solid flock of seagulls looking for food. There were people there snatching up stuff others had dumped off. Tacky furniture, books, beat-up storage bins, and stuff like that. Unless the purse was concealed thoroughly in a sturdy bag and strongly taped up, someone could have picked it up at the dump."

Shelley mused for a while. "But she was never without it. I imagine someone told Mel that."

"He knows and I told him about her being so snotty about the purse at that first luncheon. But it wouldn't hurt to remind him, I guess. I'll try to run him down when I get home."

"Why not now? I have my cell phone," Shelley said, fishing in her huge purse.

"That's your best toy, isn't it?"

"It's come in handy."

Mel was out of the office and didn't answer his own cell phone number, so Jane left the message.

"I was also wondering, if it wasn't an accident, how someone from outside the project could have come in without being noticed," Jane said.

"Good question," Shelley said. "The workers are always roaming around the whole place. If they're not looking for some tool that's been misplaced, they're gawking at what's going on elsewhere. But nothing much is going on in the kitchen right now, and it's sort of isolated. And the basement door is around a corner that isn't really obvious."

"How would anyone who didn't belong in the house get Sandra to the basement door?"

"He or she could have claimed they wanted to confide something to her privately and suggested the little hall to the basement. But only if they were familiar with the layout of the place," Shelley said.

"And almost anyone could have been. It was never locked up. I'll bet Bitsy's ex-husband had been there in the dead of night with a flashlight."

"Or Joe Budley, looking over the job he'd missed getting. In fact, it could be anyone who'd even seen the house plan for the first floor," Shelley added.

"Or some private enemy of Sandra's we don't even know about," Jane added. "She probably had a lot of them. She was a tough-minded and not especially honest or tactful person."

The waitress brought Shelley's vegetarian lasagna and Jane's spaghetti and meatballs and said with a laugh, "You're not talking about me, are you?"

"We should watch what we say in public places about this," Shelley said, picking the olives out of her salad.

18

On Monday morning Shelley called Jane early. Fortunately, Jane had been awake long enough to make some sense of what Shelley was rattling on about.

"Bitsy says she thinks she'll have the contract for us Wednesday or Thursday and she sent over the stuff we need to get into the Merchandise Mart. We can go look it over today. Are you free?"

"I guess I can be. How do we dress?"

"Like professional decorators. I'm afraid that might involve panty hose, but flat, comfortable shoes. We need to run by Bitsy's first to pick up the paperwork. Could you be ready in fifteen minutes?"

"You're not driving, right?"

"Of course not. We'll take the El and then a cab."

Jane was only five minutes over Shelley's limit. Her hair was a bit awry, but she had a brush, a mirror, and some spray in her purse and could fix it as they traveled. The slight delay allowed them to miss the worst of the rush hour, and while Jane attempted to get her hair in shape, Shelley asked, "Have you ever been to this place?"

Jane looked up. "Never."

"Me neither. I've seen it many times, but not up close. Bitsy gave us a brochure in this envelope of stuff." She glanced at Jane's hair and said, "You should stop now while you're ahead, so to speak. It looks fine."

Shelley read for a few minutes while Jane touched up her lipstick and put all her makeup and hair paraphernalia away in the oversized purse she'd chosen for this trip.

"What do you know?" Shelley said. "It was built in 1930 by Marshall Field. I had no idea it was so old. In 1945, Joseph Kennedy, of all people, bought it from Field and his estate owned it until 1995, when it was sold to a property developer."

"*That* Joseph Kennedy?"

"The very same. It's so big it has its own zip code. I think the Empire State Building does, too," Shelley said, reading on. "Dear Lord! It's twenty-seven stories high. Huge."

"Of course it's huge," Jane said. "That's why it's so famous. Does our paperwork allow us to go anywhere we want? I thought you had to be the owner or some-body really high in a decorating firm to get in at all."

"Apparently we are the president and CEO of a company from Boston," Shelley said, reading the note Bitsy had included. "I'm the president and you're the CEO."

"I don't even know what a CEO is, you realize."

"Chief executive officer. That's better than president. President is usually an honorary position and the board of directors can fire me." She thought for a moment and said, "Or maybe it's the other way around. Anyway, can you do a Boston accent?"

"We don't have to have been born and raised in Boston to live in Boston, you know. I think it would be a bit over the top to try accents," Jane said with a laugh.

Shelley's eyes got slitty with cynicism. "You know why Bitsy got us this today? Before giving us the contract?"

"To whet our appetites, right?"

"Yes. She thinks we'll be so overwhelmed by this place that we'll accept anything to come back."

Jane sighed. "She's probably right."

They were overwhelmed. They arrived at about ten-thirty and waited through a short line to be vetted and approved. They'd learned from the brochure that some of the building was open to the public and group tours, but to get into the part where real decorators could purchase items at discount rates, you had to have a letterhead document and a business tax number issued by the IRS. If you were approved, you received a clip-on identification tag you had to wear to get in. Those items were all included in the packet of paperwork Bitsy had given them.

As they inched up, Jane whispered, "What if they say we're fakes?"

"They'll probably just escort us to the front door. Trust me. I'll take care of it."

"Isn't this just as dishonest as writing term papers for other people?" Jane asked.

"Apples versus oranges, Jane. By now, if we'd had a good contract, we'd really be decorators."

There was something in this reasoning that wasn't right, Jane decided, but this was not the time to debate it.

When they reached the head of the line, Shelley casually surrendered the paperwork as if she'd done it a hundred times before and was bored senseless with the process. She turned to Jane and said, "I think we should hit the kitchen appliances first, and if there's time today, we can move to bathrooms. Next week we'll take on the wallpaper."

She spoke so confidently and bossily that the guard let them through, barely glancing at their paperwork.

For several hours they roamed around, getting lost at frequent intervals. Jane seldom bought new dishwashers and fancy plumbing for bathrooms, but Shelley seemed to have the retail prices of everything on earth in her head.

She kept hissing at Jane, "That's forty percent off retail. Boy, did I get ripped off when I replaced our bathtub." And, "Can you believe this price? It's less than half what you'd pay in a hardware or department store for this kind of toilet even if you could find one."

Contrary to the conversation at the approval stage, Shelley decided they'd look at bathroom things first. She closely examined bidets, rejecting most of them as not having attractive enough hardware. Then she moved on to a wide assortment of medicine cabinets, fancy clothes hampers, disposable Water Piks, gold-plated faucets, bath rugs, monogrammed towels in fifty colors, and an amazingly complete array of countertop ornaments, both practical and stupid. Soap holders shaped like swans, cars, treasure chests, cut-glass candy dishes, and tiny keyboards. Toothbrush holders galore, even silver-plated dental floss holders.

She looked at about forty different towel rails and decided they must have the heated kind.

"Imagine, Jane, getting out of the tub and wrapping up in a nice hot towel. You could even throw your robe over one of the heated ones before you bathe."

The only thing that really attracted Jane's attention was a shower with a computer pad that set the temperature of the water so it automatically came on right from the start.

Shelley pooh-poohed it. "Too many people are

afraid of anything computerized," she said as she moved along to a couple of dozen lavatory paper holders, toilet brush concealers, and what Jane estimated were nearly a hundred showerheads.

Jane was soon a victim of overload and sore feet. She shouldn't have brought such a big heavy purse. She kept bumping it into things and other people with it. The big purse seemed to be mysteriously gaining weight as they trudged around. But Shelley was in her element and was energized.

"I have to go home. I'm hungry. My feet hurt. I'm tired," Jane whined at 2:15.

"What a wimp you are. This is the greatest place I've ever seen. I'd camp out in one of those enormous sleigh beds we saw on our way up here for a week if they'd let me," Shelley said with a grin.

"Not me. I can find my way home and get a taxi from the train stop if you want to stay longer."

"Okay. We'll leave. But we'll come back if Bitsy comes up with a good contract. This surely has been an education. Paul told me about a place nearby that does a fabulous lunch. Come to think of it, I'm hungry, too," she said with surprise.

"Apparently neither your digestive tract nor your feet have told you what you're doing to them," Jane said, turning the wrong way to leave.

Shelley grabbed Jane's elbow. "Not that direction. Follow me."

Jane took her word for it. While Jane had been all over the world and seldom lost her bearings, the Merchandise Mart had completely destroyed her sense of direction. She obediently trailed along behind Shelley like an exhausted, whimpering puppy.

Jane recovered slightly over a Crab Louis salad, which was the best she'd ever had. "We aren't really going to do this again next week, are we?"

"We overestimated how well we had to dress," Shelley said. "Didn't you see all those people with comfy sneakers and waist packs instead of monster purses like the one you brought along? Now that we know our way around—at least *one* of us does—it'll be easier to find what we're looking for. I wish I'd ordered that salad instead of this sandwich. Let me have a bite, would you?"

"Would you be embarrassed if I took a nap on the train home?" Jane asked, gently shoving her salad plate toward Shelley.

"Only if you promise not to snore."

"I don't snore."

"How do you know?" Shelley asked.

"Well, maybe sometimes," Jane admitted. She picked at the handmade oyster crackers that had come with her salad for a moment and finally said, "Shelley, promise me you won't drag this out any further if the contract isn't really good. I'm not the same caliber of shopper that you are. You couldn't get me back into that place today if you held a gun to my temple."

"You'll get over it," Shelley said with complete confidence. "But only if we get a decent contract. I do promise you that."

19

Jane felt even worse the next morning when she woke up. The foot she had broken a bone in several months earlier, and hadn't given her so much as a twinge after she got the cast off, was slightly swollen and hurt like the devil. She was afraid she'd done it some damage and didn't even want to put shoes on today. Her left shoulder ached a bit from hauling around the heavy purse the day before.

The trip to the Merchandise Mart hadn't been good for her. She never wanted to see the place again. Of course, Shelley would go back at the drop of a hat, but Shelley really didn't need her along, regardless of the partnership. Shelley had a flair for decorating and an obsession with shopping. Jane had neither quality.

But she was good at putting colors together well, with the front hall being her single notable exception.

If the contract was good enough to accept, she'd work something out with Shelley to take less of the profits, if she herself was allowed to avoid the Merchandise Mart forevermore.

After hobbling around getting Todd and Katie off to school, she brooded over this while she soaked in a hot, sudsy bath with a paperback mystery set in an unnamed suburb of Chicago. The phone rang in her bedroom a couple of times, but she made no effort to hop out of hot soapy water to answer it.

As the water started cooling, she washed her hair, showered the soap off, put on her favorite fuzzy yellow robe and staggered out of the bathroom. The foot felt better. The shoulder no longer ached. Maybe she'd be okay.

The first message on the answering machine was Mel. He had a window of freedom at lunchtime. Did she want to eat with him? She returned his call immediately and took him up on the offer. "But let's eat here. My foot is hurting and I don't want to put on shoes."

"What did you do to it?"

"Walked seventeen miles behind Shelley yesterday at the Merchandise Mart in shoes I hadn't worn for a long time."

"Come on, Janey. Seventeen miles?"

"It seemed like it. But I have plenty of food in the house for a change. So drop by whenever you're free."

The next two calls were both from Shelley. "Where have you gone? Are you feeling better today?"

Then a little later: "I went by the House of Seven Mabels and they're tearing the sunporch down. They'll be starting a replacement tomorrow. Bitsy's trying to save a bit of money by making it smaller, but I think she's wrong. I need you to back me up before they pour the new foundations. If she's going to have a sunporch, it needs to be generous. Or she shouldn't replace it at all. Oh, and Bitsy still doesn't have the new contract. I can see that your car's in the garage. Why are you hiding out?"

Shelley was the only person she knew who could conduct an entire conversation with an answering machine.

Jane returned the call. "My foot hurts again and so did my shoulder, so I was taking a long, hot bath," Jane told her.

"What did you do to your foot?"

"Walked around behind you. I'm not even putting shoes on today."

"Oh, Jane. I'm so sorry. I wouldn't have hauled you along if I'd known that would happen."

"Mel's coming over later. I'm making deviled ham sandwiches. Give me ten or fifteen minutes so I can dress, and keep me entertained while I work on them."

"You want me to do it for you? You should have your foot up, not walking around the kitchen."

"It's my secret recipe. I have to do it myself. And the foot is feeling better."

Jane threw on jeans and a T-shirt and ran a comb through her hair. That last haircut was worth paying a fortune for at the day spa. She didn't even have to blow-dry it. It just fell into place. The investment had paid off.

She was doing a rough chop of the ham in the Cuisinart when Shelley showed up with a handful of paperwork. "Your hair looks great. I may have to try out that day spa myself. Want me to start your coffee?"

"Oh, please do."

"Bitsy says the contract's almost okay," Shelley said as she worked. "Bitsy will supply the digital camera. She'll give us an advance on the furnishings she approves from the pictures. She's willing to give us a ten percent commission on the receipts we file. It's not enough. I'm going to see if I can bump that up to seventeen and a half percent. It's a fair amount and she'll still be getting a bargain on everything. I've checked around and I think it's a reasonable commission."

Jane sighed as she started putting exactly the right amount of finely chopped red pepper into the mix. "Shelley, I'm sick at heart to leave you high and dry, but I simply can't face that place again."

"The Merchandise Mart, you mean? I already knew that. I've never seen you look so drained and pathetic. I'll do it myself and consult with you over the pictures I take before I show our choices to Bitsy. I don't mind a bit if you'll take care of the color combinations. You're far better at that than I am."

"In spite of my turning the front hall into a dungeon?"

"Your only mistake," Shelley said generously. "Could have happened to anyone. I thought it was going to look good, too. What's that you're putting in that ham now?"

"A tiny breath of curry powder. Then I mix it with mayo. Spread it generously on toasted slices of baguettes just before serving."

"Sounds divine. What are you having with it?"

"I thought about an egg salad, but it's too much like the texture of the ham. Maybe a really big hearty spinach salad with onions and bacon and just a few chopped eggs."

"Excellent choice. I'll get the eggs boiling for you and wash the spinach. Are you going to gird your loins—I've always wondered what that really means— and ask Mel about the investigation into Sandra's death? Has he found out anything about her?"

"He hasn't said. I'll test the waters," Jane said, putting the ham mixture in a bowl and adding the mayo. "If he's still cranky, I'll let it go for now and catch him when he's not so busy."

"Go sit down in the living room and get that foot up on a chair. I'll put everything away in the fridge for now and you can finish it up later."

Jane took her advice and settled in on the sofa with her right foot up on the back of it. Shelley had been right. She shouldn't have walked around on it. She asked Shelley to go upstairs and find the mystery she'd been reading. "I think I left it in the bathroom."

Shelley brought it down. "It's a little damp, I'm afraid. I'll leave you alone until after Mel's gone. Is it okay if I tell Bitsy you agree with me about the size of the sunporch?"

"I do agree. If she's going to replace it, she should do it right or not do it."

Mel was impressed with lunch in spite of his saying it was a girly choice. But awfully good and filling. "Sorry I've been such a crank for the last week, Janey. Having to cover the rock concert and then this damned house the next day put me over the edge."

"I understand. How'd you get away today?"

"I delegated."

"*You* delegated?" Jane said with a laugh. "I thought you didn't believe in ever doing that."

"I don't, but I'm giving it a try. Comes from getting older and more tired, I guess. Go out to the living room and put your bad foot back up. Shouldn't you have it X-rayed again?"

"I'll see what a day off it does before I put myself through that again. I don't ever want to be in a cast for the rest of my life."

Mel graciously loaded the dishwasher for her. Of

course she'd have to redo it when he was gone. There was something genetic about men that didn't let them understand why glassware really should go on the top rack. Her late husband had once gone through a brief spell when she was pregnant with Todd when he was trying to be helpfully domestic and cracked several pieces of her favorite glassware from the drying process. She'd never let Mike load it, and Todd could do so only with Katie's supervision.

When Mel was through, he came and sat at the far end of the sofa and massaged her good foot. The massage made even the bad one feel better.

Since he was mellowed out by lunch and delegating, she asked, "Have you found out anything about Sandra's background?"

"A little bit. It was hard to trace her. The name change wasn't official. She'd just decided to take back her mother's maiden name."

"Shelley and I had the impression that she had been married. When we met her the first time, Bitsy said something about her once being Mrs. Somebody. They seemed to make a joke of it. So she was once married?"

"Yes. To a man who severely abused her, to the point that she was hospitalized several times. Makes you understand why she became such a rabid feminist, I have to admit."

"Do you know where he is? Could he have found her and killed her?"

"No. He's serving a life sentence for murdering his third wife and their two-year-old child. He beat them to death two years ago."

Jane suddenly hurt all over.

The phone rang, and Mel looked at Jane's shocked face and said, "I'll get it for you."

"Yes," he said when he answered. "This is Van-Dyne."

A moment of silence and then he said, "Hell. I'm just a short distance away. I'll be there in a few minutes."

"What is it, Mel?" Jane called to him.

"I left your number at the office. It seems that they've found an unknown toolbox at that damned house and somebody thinks there's a bomb in it."

20

Mel was standing with the others who'd been evacuated from the house and neighboring homes to the parking lot of a church down the street. It had turned into an unusually hot day, and the neighbors wanted to go home. The mothers with babies had commandeered the only shade available under an old maple tree at the far end of the parking area.

"Mr. Budley," Mel said, "it seems to me that the last time we spoke, you were explaining how well you'd sealed up the house. Now there's a toolbox in the basement that no one recognizes. How do you explain this? Who has the keys?"

"I can't explain it except that it could have been there for days and your people missed it."

"My 'people' don't miss things," Mel said firmly.

"As for the keys, all the doors that can be locked are keyed the same. Only the owner and I have copies," Budley said. He was insisting on taking the high ground on this matter.

Budley walked away, and Mel realized that the young woman who worked on the Sheetrock had been waiting to speak to him.

"Detective VanDyne," Evaline said. "I'm sorry to tell you this, but there's something else you should know that I didn't hear Joe Budley mention. Whoever got in the house also took a hammer to the Sheetrock upstairs. Bashed it pretty badly. We can probably patch a few of the dents, but several sheets will have to be replaced."

"How do you know it was the same person?" Mel asked.

"I guess I don't," Evaline said with a shrug. "I just assumed that since the house has been locked up, but somebody found a way in."

As they were speaking, the bomb squad started drifting out of the house. One had a plastic bag that was obviously heavy. The two others were taking off their protective clothing and hoods.

Mel abandoned Evaline and hurried to meet them.

"It's okay, Mel," the man carrying the bag said, lifting his mask. "It did look like a bomb, but it's just a bunch of junk stuck together with a clock attached that doesn't even work. No explosives. You can give the box to the fingerprint people," he added, handing Mel the bag.

"How did it get in there? Do you have any idea?"

"That paneling on the back wall conceals the door to an old coal chute. It was ajar when we went down there. I don't think you could have seen it if it had been closed. You better fingerprint it as well," the man replied as he struggled out of his modern armor. His clothing under it was drenched with sweat.

That eased Mel's mind. He'd looked over every inch of the basement and hadn't noticed anything odd about the paneling except that it was cheap and ugly. If he himself hadn't noticed, he could hardly go back to the station and tear holes in the other investigators of the basement.

He went back and reassured the crowd that they could go home now and that it hadn't been a bomb, only a fake one. But he made a point of snagging Joe Budley. "Mr. Budley, you can let your workers back in, but not anywhere near the basement or the backyard."

"But we've need to get the footings in for the sunporch today or we'll be a whole day late."

"That's at the other end of the house, right?"

"It is."

"Then we'll let them work. But there will be a police tape at the north end that you're responsible for making sure they don't cross. By the way, I'm wondering why you didn't tell me about the damage to the Sheetrock."

"What damage?"

"Evaline told me someone had taken a hammer to it."

"Why didn't anyone tell *me* this?" Budley exclaimed.

"You didn't know?" Mel said, not believing him.

"I hadn't yet been upstairs today. I was working with the guys who are replacing the sunporch. Why didn't Evaline or Carl tell me?"

"Maybe they hoped you wouldn't found out."

"I'd have known when they billed me for fixing it. I'm going to have a talk with them."

"You're going to have to shut down the work upstairs until I get my staff back. And Evaline and Carl have probably already destroyed the evidence by fixing it."

This, unfortunately, made Budley smile.

Mel walked around the back of the house, keeping a safe distance so he wouldn't disturb any footprints. He guessed that the coal chute must have once come out where there were now some very old shrubs. He made some phone calls and was told that the photographer from the police department who'd taken the photos at the scene of Sandra's death revealed something interesting.

"Mel, Phil here," the photographer said. "I thought you should know. When I developed the pictures, I saw something strange that wasn't visible in the gloom down there but showed up in the flash."

"I bet I know what it was. A piece of that dreadful paneling that looked very slightly different?"

"How'd you guess?"

"It's covering an old coal chute. The bomb squad boys said it was ajar. I've sealed off where it must exit and having the toolbox brought in for prints."

"What do you bet there aren't any? Is everything in it new?"

"I haven't looked in the bag yet. I don't want anything to contaminate it, but I'd bet the same. I'll bring it in as soon as the fingerprint group gets here. And you might mention that the scene-of-the-crime group should bring along some big loppers to cut down some ugly old shrubs and take them away to test for fibers."

He called back to the station and told his assistants about the Sheetrock and that they would to have to come back. That news wasn't received well.

Mel was sweating nearly as much as the bomb squad person had and wanted nothing more than to go home and shower, but he stuck it out, without ever letting go of the bag containing the toolbox until everyone he'd called up had arrived and had their instructions. His arm was sore from the weight of the contents.

When he had it stowed in the trunk of his car, he called Jane and assured her he hadn't been in any danger because the bomb was a fake. "Now go back to your sofa and put your foot back up," he said, still in police mode.

"Yes, sir," she replied.

"*Please* put your foot back up," he added, realizing how sharply he'd spoken.

Jane didn't mention that she hadn't been on the

sofa anyway. She was propped up in bed changing channels on the television to distract herself. Or had been until Shelley snatched the control from her hand and turned it off a moment before Mel called.

"What?" Shelley said the minute Jane hung up.

"The bomb was a fake. That's all he said."

"So what was the 'yes, sir' about?"

"He told me in his police voice to put my foot up," Jane said with a smile.

"Jane, I don't get this. It turns our theories inside out. I really thought all this stuff like the rotten shrimp and the other vandalism was to persecute Sandra."

Jane nodded. "So did I, I suppose. So why this fake bomb scare? Why not a real bomb? And to what purpose?"

"That gets us back to Bitsy's ex-husband, persecuting her, I'd guess."

"I don't know if that's true. If he had the kind of connections to hire someone sleazy, he'd have them plant a real bomb, wouldn't he?"

"Who could tell?" Shelley said. "Except for Sandra's death, which could—barely could, I should say—be an accident, nobody's been hurt seriously by any of this. Even Jacqueline wouldn't have been knocked out except that she jumped back from the plug, fell, and hit her head."

Before leaving the scene, Mel went upstairs to survey the damage to the Sheetrock. Sure enough, most of it was already contaminated by Carl and Evaline's having already patched up most of the damage. Budley was standing in the middle of the room, arms crossed and glaring around the room. "You'd have thought they'd of had the sense to tell me about this. I wish I'd never taken on this job."

"I wish I hadn't been assigned to it," Mel admitted.

As he was approaching his car, the scene-of-the-crime crew showed up again. Mel left instructions as to where a coal chute must have come out. "It's concealed with a nasty bank of prickly shrubs you're going to have to cut down. But look carefully for anything fresh that's snagged in them."

By the time Mel got back to the station, he had a call from the head of the group. "We found mostly animal fur. But there were a few bits of plain white cottony paper. The sort of stuff you'd find in those outfits that painters sometimes wear. Available at almost any hardware store. The lab will have to confirm this, of course. No fingerprints inside or out."

"I guess I should be thanking you for this information, but I can't bring myself to do so. Sounds to me like we're striking out again."

21

A day staying off her foot made Jane a new woman. She'd gone out to the garage and found one of the old crutches so she could move around a little without touching her right foot to the floor. By evening, she could honestly report to Shelley and Mel that she didn't need to go back to the hospital to have it X-rayed again.

Mel dropped by to check on her after dinner and asked if there was any kind of dessert around.

"Just grocery-store cookies. But even Shelley says they're edible. Finish them off before I have to."

He sat down with a glass of milk, polished off the last three cookies, and sighed. "I'm sick to death of that house of Bitsy's. It's been three weeks."

"It hasn't," Jane said with a laugh.

"Okay. Maybe a week, but it seems like a lot longer. And there's still no irrefutable evidence of a serious crime."

"Not even Sandra's death?"

"Except for her missing purse, there's nothing solid to make anyone think it was murder. It could have just been an accident."

"It's more than the purse, Mel. She was disliked by nearly everyone working for her. And who knows how many other people she's crossed paths with who had even better reason to hate her."

"But Jane, the world's full of obnoxious people who irritate the hell out everyone and nobody murders them. They just get older and more obnoxious. I have an eighty-four-year-old great-uncle who's a living example."

"Didn't the bomb scare count as a crime?" Jane asked.

"Only marginally. It wasn't a real bomb. If we knew who did it and were in England, we could get him or her for 'wasting police time.' The rest of it could count merely as damaging pranks. Even that would be cause only for a lawsuit, not a criminal conviction."

"It wasn't Thomasina's missing toolbox, I assume?"

"No. Hers was a big yellow plastic one," Mel said. "The one in the basement was steel."

Jane brushed the cookie crumbs onto a napkin she wadded up to throw away later. "The thing I don't understand is why the pranks have continued beyond Sandra's death—whatever the cause of it. I assumed they were all aimed at discrediting her, but now it looks as if Bitsy's the target."

"I suspect you're right, but again, there's no proof of it."

"What about her ex-husband?"

"He's sleaze," Mel said, getting up and roaming fretfully around the kitchen as if looking for a solution—perhaps under the morning paper on the counter or under a pot. "And he makes no attempt to disguise his contempt for her. And it's rumored that some of his clients are big-money mafia. But it's only rumor and we don't have any evidence that would allow us to get at his records. Even if we did, he's bright enough not to leave evidence of personal conversations in his files."

"Have you interviewed any of Sandra's friends from her feminist group?"

"Dozens. The most hostile group of women I've come across. They regard her as a saint."

"To be a real saint, you have to be dead," Jane said. "I wonder if they thought so when she was alive. Oh, I never thought to ask. Did you check the dust marks on the steps to the basement?"

Mel just stared at her for a long moment. "First pictures taken. And somebody with far too much free time had recently swept them. The only thing on the steps was a bit of mud from the shoe of the doctor who pronounced her dead."

Jane stared back. "Don't you think that's odd?"

"Of course it's odd. There was a broom down there. And before you ask the obvious question, yes, it was fingerprinted and was absolutely clear of prints."

"You don't really think this was an accident, do you," Jane said.

"I don't think it for a moment, but I can't disprove it, either." His pager beeped and he said, "It's forensics. May I use your phone? My cell phone's gone all staticky and someone in the office is trying to replace it and get the same number."

When he returned the call, he kept nodding and looking glummer by the minute. Hanging up, he said, "The scene-of-the-crime guys were right. The only new stuff on the damned bushes was a paper-based substance with a few threads. From a coverall that's sold in, oh, maybe a thousand paint and hardware stores just in the Chicago area alone."

"No fingerprints?" Jane asked.

"Do you have any idea how common latex or plastic gloves are? You can get them in most drugstores, even if you have to purchase a box of hair color. Even more easily in paint and hardware stores. I liked the good old days when gloves were leather or fabric. At least they'd sometimes leave some kind of print or evidence. I guess I'm just going to have to start another whole round of interviews tomorrow and see if there's any triviality we've missed. Do you mind if I skip out on you and spend what's left of the evening going over what I already have so far?"

"I don't. But I wish I could help. Shelley and I know the workers on a more friendly basis than you do. We haven't a clue in spite of that, except the missing purse. I can't remember if I told you that when we first met Sandra it was at a restaurant and she had it slung across her shoulder and never turned loose of it. She even got her fork tangled in the strap, but didn't let it go. I thought even then it was sort of odd.

"When most women eat out, they set it next to them. And when they're working at an office or job site, they lock it up somewhere. Under the seat of their car sometimes. Or in a drawer to which they have the only key. But Sandra never let hers leave her body."

"Maybe she was one of those people who always carried a whole lot of cash around," Mel speculated.

Jane shook her head. "In my experience traveling with my parents all over the world, my folks always had paper money concealed in a thin pack tied underneath their clothing. I don't think it was cash she was protecting."

"Then what would a woman keep in a purse that she couldn't keep in such a pack?" Mel asked.

Jane shrugged. "Drugs? A notebook of important data? A datebook? A weapon such as a sharp knife or gun?"

After Mel had gone, Jane called Shelley. "Come on

over if you're free. We need to toss around some ideas about the missing purse."

When Shelley arrived, she said, "You know, I just realized it wasn't always the same purse."

"No?"

"She had two in the same style. One was a dark blue or black. The other was the exact same style, but in a sort of dark taupe. She must have been concerned about being color savvy," Shelley said.

"I think you're right. She had the dark one at the restaurant and the brownish one that she normally had strapped across her chest at work. I hadn't realized that until you mentioned it. But, Shelley, neither of them was huge. Large, but not the enormous sort of thing you'd take on a plane with all your medications, a change of underwear, makeup, mouthwash, and your jewelry bag, in case the checked luggage didn't show up."

Shelley grinned at the image. "I traveled with Paul and his assistant once on a flight. I had my laptop, a camera bag, and the huge kind of purse you're talking about. The assistant had a laptop, a camera bag, and a backpack smaller than my purse, and they forced him to check through the backpack. Sort of reverse sexual harassment, I thought. I kept my purse in my lap, but they wouldn't let him keep the backpack in his lap."

"You're kidding," Jane said with a laugh.

"So what do you want to talk about regarding Sandra's purse?"

Jane went over the conversation she and Mel had had. "It was strange to see a woman who never, ever turned loose of her purse, even when she was eating. It was obvious that she had something in it that was so valuable to her that she was never without it literally wrapped around her. I'm always losing track of mine. I dump it in the kitchen when I come home, or sometimes I carry it upstairs with me or toss it on a sofa."

"What do you suppose she did with it at night?" Shelley asked.

"Probably chained it to the bedpost or kept it in a safe," Jane suggested. "So what was in it that was so important?"

"A weapon?"

"Mel and I considered that. We also considered that she was one of those people who always felt compelled to have a lot of ready cash on hand, but when I traveled with my parents we always had our paper cash strapped under our clothes."

"Did you consider drugs?"

"First on the list. That's the only thing I think someone would steal the purse for. We also thought about a datebook and one of those big address books, but I don't think the purses were big enough for those things."

"Where's your own purse right now?" Shelley asked.

"I have no idea," Jane said.

Shelley found it in the squashy chair in the living

room. Jane started taking things out. "Billfold. Sun-glasses case. A paperback book in the side pocket in case I get trapped with nothing to read. Checkbook. A packet of tissues. A box of wintergreen Altoids. Breath spray. Some loose change in the bottom, two ballpoint pens, a pencil. A few crumpled receipts. Some dust-balls. Hmm. A dead leaf? How did that get in here?"

"What about the little inside zippered pocket?"

"A pair of manicure scissors. A nail file. Lipstick. Yet another pen. A six-inch piece of yellow ribbon."

"What's that for?"

"A craft project Katie wanted to do. I was supposed to find a match for this ribbon."

"I'll bet mine has the same kind of things, plus the cell phone and maybe a little box of aspirin."

"This purse is about the same size as hers. So what made it worth stealing and presumably disposing of?"

22

Mel called Jane the next morning. "Thought you'd like to know that the mystery purse has reappeared," he said in a weary voice. "And before you ask, there are no fingerprints, inside or out."

"You mean it was empty?" Jane asked.

"No, everything you'd normally expect was there. Lipstick, comb, billfold with several credit cards and around seventy dollars in cash and change. A pack of tissues, her cell phone. That sort of thing."

"Nothing unusual?"

"What would you consider unusual?"

"I don't know. A length of yellow ribbon?" Jane said, thinking back to the examination of her own purse contents.

"No. Would that mean something of significance I'm not aware of?"

"Uh-huh. It's just that Shelley and I went through my purse and I had a piece of yellow ribbon in it."

"Why?"

Jane sighed. "It doesn't matter. I was just trying to match it for Katie. The point is that I had to explain to Shelley why I was carrying it around."

Mel didn't reply. She could almost hear him making a silly face.

"Where was it found?" she asked.

"That's the interesting thing. It was in a paper bag, also with no prints. I absolutely hate the ease of getting disposable latex gloves."

"But where?"

"Sitting on the newly poured concrete on the sunporch. The concrete had been heavily salted."

"Salted?"

"Yes, apparently that wrecks the surface. Budley is furious. It's going to have to be all be torn out, taken to the dump, and done again, destroying his schedule and raising the cost at his expense."

"Why at his expense?"

"Because your friend Bitsy got a bid from him and locked him into the amount and the timing. With a hefty penalty for every day late to finish the project."

"Wow! She finally got a good lawyer to draw it up."

Mel wasn't interested in this aspect. "When the first workers arrived, they didn't even noticed the pitting of the surface until they tried to throw the paper bag away and the bottom stuck to the surface and there sat the purse. Thank God nobody touched it."

Jane dragged herself back to thinking about the purse.

"Mel, were there any receipts in the purse or billfold?"

"Not a one. Why do you ask?"

"Nor a notebook or note cards for writing things down? Like a shopping list?"

Mel was slow to reply. "No," he finally said. "Janey, thanks for thinking of that."

"Do you think it means something?"

"It might," he admitted. "A purse is a bit like a man's jacket pockets or billfold, I imagine. I'm always finding notes to myself and beat-up receipts when I take a jacket to the cleaners or my billfold starts bulging. I have to go. I'm glad I filled you in on what's going on. Your take on things is interesting."

"You've never admitted that before."

"Why would I?"

"Just to be nice," Jane said with a laugh. "Like you are today."

"Only today?" he asked. "It's probably just because she was overorganized about keeping her purse free of debris." Before she could reply to his attempt to back out of the compliment he'd given her, he said, "I have someone here who wants to talk to me. See you later."

Jane picked up her own purse from the kitchen

chair where she'd put it and discovered a side pocket she and Shelley had overlooked. It contained a paper clip, yet another ballpoint pen, and two very old grocery lists written on scraps of paper, one sheet apparently torn from a blank page in the back of an old paperback book.

She threw these away and called Shelley.

"We got a compliment from Mel a few minutes ago. On a purely domestic thing I mentioned we'd done."

"Do tell!" Shelley exclaimed.

"His call was about finding the purse that's been missing."

She recounted what he'd said about the contents and what questions she'd asked, leaving out the concrete problem for the moment.

"Jane, he's never really appreciated our views before, you know. It's terrific that he finally realizes that we know ordinary everyday domestic things that might be important."

"To be honest, Shelley, he tried to weasel out of having admitted that, then cut me off to talk to someone else."

"Of course he did. He's a man, after all," Shelley advised. "I assume they found it outdoors."

"Why would you assume that?" Jane asked. Shelley had spoiled her next bit of information.

"Because Bitsy had all the locks changed. And Budley, you, and I have the only duplicates. One of the four of us must show up early every morning from now on to let the workers in."

"It's not going to be me, and it shouldn't be you. We're not being paid, or even contracted to be paid yet."

"Good point."

"Besides, she didn't give me a key," Jane continued.

"She gave me yours. This was the first chance I've had to pass it along. So where was the purse found?"

Jane told her.

"More vandalism," Shelley said with a sigh. "I'm starting to wonder all over again if Sandra really was murdered. Nothing else that's happened actually hurt anyone."

"The planer hurt Jacqueline," Jane argued.

"But only because she jumped back and hit her head against something. It wasn't meant to harm her, according to Thomasina."

Shelley went on. "All the other of the catastrophes are just nasty. The damage to the Sheetrock, the shrimp in the furnace pipes—excluding, of course, the two women who were nauseated. The salting of the fresh concrete and the fake bomb in the toolbox are other good examples. They all merely caused trouble and delays."

"Even if nobody was seriously hurt, the next such incident might go awry," Jane objected. "And anyone working there or even sneaking onto the site will probably go on doing things until they get their way."

"Say that again."

Jane repeated her statement.

"That could be what it's all really about," Shelley said. "Who stands to profit by this? Bitsy's ex-husband? Just to destroy her project that he thinks he's actually paying for out of the divorce settlement? Or Joe Budley, who ended up with a job he seemed to have needed?"

"Shelley, that doesn't make sense anymore, unfortunately. I can see that he might have tried to sabotage the job to get Sandra fired, so he got a second shot at making money on Bitsy. But why would he continue?"

"Just to cover his own ass, Jane."

"I don't think so. Mel told me something else I almost forgot to tell you. He says Budley's furious because Bitsy made him sign a contract that specifies penalties if he doesn't finish it at the bid he gave and on the date he set for completion."

"Uh-oh. Bitsy got herself a good lawyer at last."

"Exactly what I thought."

"She's probably running my version of *our* contract by him, too."

"Oh. That's true. Honestly, Shelley, I hope he tears it to pieces. We don't really want to do this job, do we?"

"I'd still enjoy the shopping part," Shelley said with a slight whine in her voice. "And I'd like to be a part of the end result. But not if a savvy attorney gets involved."

"I guess we'll see. I didn't get a chance to ask Mel something I'm wondering about, now that I think about it. I asked what was in the purse. And he said everything you'd expect to find. But when I asked if she had a notebook or any receipts or scraps of paper with notes or lists, he said no. That's what he was complimenting us for thinking of."

"So what did you forget to ask?"

"Whether they'd found a filing system at her house. I assume they searched it pretty thoroughly for clues about her life. He mentioned that maybe she was just too organized to carry trash around in her purse."

"You have to catch up with him and find out," Shelley said.

"I guess I do. So, do we have anything else we really need to do today? I'd like to stay home, go back over the book, and make changes now that I know what Priscilla's house looks like."

"I don't think we need to go over there again until we find out about the contract," Shelley said. "But just in case we get what we want, there's something I'd like to do this evening."

Jane was immediately wary. There was something odd about the way Shelley spoke. "And what is that?"

"It's a full moon tonight and it's supposed to be a really clear night."

"So?"

"Well, I thought since we have a key, we could go over and see what the House of Seven Mabels looks like at night. All those windows and skylights. Just to fuel our imaginations, you see. It may change our minds about color schemes."

Jane didn't like the idea, but said, "I suppose we could. I know from your tone of voice that you're going to do it whether I go along or not. And I don't want you in that place all by yourself, but I'd like to get Mel to come along to protect us."

"He wouldn't go along with that, do you think?"

"Maybe. I'll see."

To Jane's surprise, Mel agreed. "I don't want you two roaming around there when it's empty. Besides, it might provide me with something I've missed."

They met at the front door at nine. Shelley and Jane had stayed in Jane's car until Mel arrived. It turned out that he had a key of his own that Bitsy hadn't mentioned.

"There seem to be a great many more keys floating around than we thought," Jane mentioned in passing to Shelley in an undertone.

Mel also had a flashlight to lead them upstairs. He kept it carefully aimed at the floor.

When they got into the part of the house that was being renovated, Shelley pointed first to the skylight over the door to the area. "Hmm," she said.

"Hmm, indeed," Mel said, looking up. "I don't think that's the Northern Lights."

Jane looked up. The sky, instead of being the clear white of a full moon, was faintly pink.

Mel said, "Stay right where you are," in a voice that couldn't be argued with. He went to one of the back windows. "There's a fire out back" was all he said before asking Shelley for her cell phone to call the fire department.

23

Mel had Jane and Shelley out of the house, into Jane's car, and on their way home before the first fire truck arrived. He wasn't about to admit to anyone that he was there simply to help out the decorators in his free time. With them gone, he could justifiably say he was checking out the house, just being a good cop on his *own* time.

He called Jane a short while later from his apartment. "Sorry I was so curt. I had no idea if there was something in the Dumpster that could explode," he lied. "But whoever did this put only a pint or two of kerosene in the far end. The fire probably could have been doused with a pitcher of water instead of three fire engines."

"So, just one more little nasty trick?"

"Not necessarily," Mel said. "If we hadn't happened to be there to notice, it might have burned to the other end of the Dumpster and generated enough heat and flame to burn the whole place down."

"Am I to understand that you're saying it was a good thing we dragged you over there?" Jane asked.

"I guess it was," Mel admitted.

"Any hints of who did it?"

"Nope. No container left behind. And the ground around the far end is so compacted it won't take footprints. Janey, you're not really going to take this job, are you?"

"I hope not," Jane said. "Shelley's excited about the shopping possibilities and I'd hate to let her down. But Bitsy seems to have found a good attorney who probably won't approve the contract Shelley drew up. That's about the only thing that could get me off the hook. You want to come by for glass of wine?"

"Thanks, but I've had a very long day. How about tomorrow?"

"That sounds fine. Are you going to suggest to Bitsy that she hire some security people?"

"I already called and reported the fire to her and suggested it," Mel said, his voice fading with weariness. "She says she doesn't think she can afford it. So much has already gone wrong and it's costing her much more than she planned, she says."

"She has a point. But I worry that the next little trick might actually harm or kill someone."

"So do I." His words ended in a yawn. "Janey, I'm falling into bed in three seconds."

"Sleep well," Jane said softly.

She rang up Shelley to report what Mel had told her.

"I'm glad we were there before it got out of hand," Shelley said.

"Why are you talking funny?" Jane asked.

"I'm putting this new gunk I bought for wrinkles on my face and I don't want to get it all over the phone," she explained.

"Did you get me some, too?"

"I did. I'll give you your bottle tomorrow."

"Do you still want to go on with this job?" Jane asked.

"The wrinkle project? Of course."

"No, I mean the House of Seven Mabels." Jane realized she'd fallen into Shelley's habit of calling it that.

"I've been thinking about it," Shelley said thoughtfully. "I wish Bitsy would hop to it and show us the revised contract. If it's too good to pass up, which I doubt, we'd make a lot of money to spend on ourselves."

Jane was silent for a moment. Shelley's husband made tons of money and wasn't the least bit stingy with it. So that wasn't the real reason Shelley was sticking with this idiocy. Jane wondered if Shelley truly looked forward to the whole shopping thing that much or if she was doing it for her. Jane was comfortable with her income from the pharmacies but probably could be more financially secure with a real job and more money. Was that on Shelley's mind as well?

"I guess we'll just have to see what happens next," Jane said. "You don't suppose Bitsy would ever consider just giving this up and selling it back to the township to tear down?"

"I wouldn't think so," Shelley said. "Think of all the costs she's already paid. I think she'll hold out to the bitter end."

"Unless—"

"Unless what?"

"I can hardly bear to say it, but if she's insured the project, she might be better off if it had burned down tonight."

The silence now was on Shelley's end. Finally she said, "It's possible. She's changed a lot in the years we weren't in touch with her. I bet she hasn't bought so much as a single roll of crepe paper in five years. Who knows how desperate she is to close this bad experience? It's worth thinking about. Has Mel ever mentioned the possibility?"

"Not to me," Jane said. "But maybe I'll suggest he give it some thought."

Jane could hardly get to sleep that night. She tried forcing herself to think about the book she was writing and what Priscilla would do next. But her thoughts kept coming back to Bitsy. She'd never seriously suspected Bitsy until a second before she spoke the words to Shelley. If Sandra's death was an accident, which she didn't think for a moment, then what was the point of all the nasty pranks afterward?

Maybe it really did come back to Bitsy's ex-husband. The single time she'd seen him, Jane had taken an instant and intense dislike to him. He'd been clearly gloating over Bitsy's apparent failure to get on with the job. Was it possible he had nothing to do with Sandra's death, but was responsible for the other incidents?

The house had been fully accessible to anyone who wanted to get in to put the shrimp in the ducts. He could have done it or hired someone to do it for him. After Joe Budley took over as contractor and the locks were changed and windows boarded up, the "pranks" took place outside. Salting the concrete. Starting the fire.

But if Budley had nothing to do with Sandra's death, who climbed through the dense shrubs, went down the virtually invisible coal chute, and brought the purse back?

As she thought back, she was wrong. The toolbox with the fake bomb showed up in the house, and so did Sandra's purse, *after* Budley took over.

Did it really have to be one and only one person? Or was it some sort of conspiracy? Maybe even several people, unknown to each other, grinding their own axes?

———

When Shelley and Jane had both finished their morning car pools, Jane went over to Shelley's house with a legal pad and pen. "We're going to make a timeline. Maybe that will show us something we've forgotten."

But Shelley sidetracked her with the anti-wrinkle cream. "Try it."

"Not now. I've already put my makeup on."

"No, you haven't."

"I thought I had," Jane said, trying to remember the morning rush. The kids had both gotten up late and both their schools took tardiness seriously. "Smells good," she said, rubbing a little bit of it under her eyes.

"They say within a week you'll see a difference. If this house thing doesn't pan out, maybe we could become reps and sell the stuff," Shelley said with a laugh.

"Yeah, right. Door to door, I assume. No thank you."

"So, we're making another of your legendary lists?" Shelley asked. It was a running joke. Jane was a compulsive list maker.

"Not exactly a list. More like a couple of charts. Okay, let's start with everyone involved in the renovation and what we know about them. First is Bitsy. I'll make a note across from her name regarding possible motives. An insurance scam, for one."

"Don't you need another column for reasons these people *aren't* the ones responsible?" Shelley suggested.

"Good idea. See? You're already contributing. We mark Bitsy as the one who stands to profit the most in the last column."

"Are you considering Sandra?"

"I suppose we could list her, but she was already dead before most of the things happened."

"Put her down anyway. The object is to be thorough, right? To jar us into some conclusions or things to find out."

Jane put Sandra's name down. Under Sandra, she also added the thugs who collected the rents for the previous owners. Not by name, of course.

"We know nothing about them and never will," Shelley objected.

"But they could be behind everything that's happened. Wanting to get their lucrative jobs back."

Shelley just shrugged. "It's your list."

"Jacqueline Hunt is next. What motive could she have?"

"None," Shelley said. "She was one of the victims, remember. She got a shock when she plugged in the planer."

"That doesn't necessarily exclude her from things that happened later. Maybe revenge for someone she thought set her up for the shock."

"Jane, don't you think it's unlikely that several people are vandalizing the house and endangering others?"

"Unlikely, but possible. Just go with the flow, Shelley. If we're wasting time, we'll know it when we get the charts done."

"Charts? Plural?" Shelley groaned.

"The second one is going to be the order bad things happened. So we'll put possible revenge for getting shocked."

"Jane, that doesn't make sense. Which stunt do you imagine she did? It could only be some of them aimed at Bitsy. Jacqueline is proud of her work and certainly would want to see it completed. She's also making money from Bitsy. Why would she jeopardize a good job?"

"Okay, okay," Jane said grumpily. "I'll cross out revenge. I guess we mark nothing for Henrietta Smith, either. You could say the same for her. They work as a pair. What about Wesley Woodly, the furnace guy? He certainly had nothing but contempt for both Bitsy and Sandra."

"But the furnace and air conditioning are working now. And he's been paid and is no longer on the job. Why would he care what happens to the project?" Shelley objected again.

"Because there's the other side of the upstairs still to be done and the whole downstairs. He's only temporarily off the job. Maybe he's so desperate to avoid coming back, he'd sabotage the whole deal," Jane said smugly.

"I'll reluctantly give you that one."

"Will you also give me the two women who were throwing up in the front yard?"

"No."

"Okay. Then we come to my favorite. Bitsy's ex-husband, Neville."

"Put him down," Shelley said. "He's got the best motive to wreck Bitsy's project. A man scorned, and thinking it's really his hard-earned money that's funding this project. Now, are we done with this chart?"

"We've hardly begun," Jane said.

Shelley put her head down on the kitchen table and pretended to weep.

24

Next are the people doing the Sheetrock. Carl Stringfield."

"We know nothing about him. We've only been introduced to him once," Shelley countered.

"So he's blank for now. But we need to speak to him. Or find out about him from Evaline. She's next on the list, and we know a lot about her."

"She did term papers for other people," Shelley huffed. "I don't know if that's illegal, but it's immoral."

"We've been through that already. But she's one of the brightest, most competent, and most imaginative of any of them—as far as we know."

"But what would be her motive? You're back to what we said about Jacqueline and Henry. She's landed a job she's good at and being paid for. Besides, she and Carl are victims, too. Someone wrecked their work and they had to do it again."

"Okay, okay. You're right again. But we have to list them. And now another of my favorites. Joe Budley."

"That jerk," Shelley said. "Yes, put him down. But as much as I dislike him, I don't think he's responsible for the things that have happened since he took the job as contractor. There's nothing in it for him. Quite the contrary. If what we've heard is true, he has a deadline and a budget he has to adhere to."

"But he could have been the one who planted the shrimp and niggled with the wiring before Sandra died. He might even be the one who killed Sandra. Didn't Thomasina say he really wanted that job before Bitsy got tangled up with Sandra?"

"That's true, I guess. But you can't imagine he'd sabotage himself." Shelley got up from her kitchen table and started to unload the dishwasher.

"We're back to having two or more suspects," Jane said, feeling discouraged.

"I find that hard to imagine," Shelley said, stacking plates. "My money's still on Bitsy's ex-husband."

"I guess the last on the list is Thomasina, the electrician. Suppose she herself accidentally made the wiring error that resulted in Jacqueline being knocked out?"

"Interesting question," Shelley admitted, almost

dropping a handful of spoons. "She might have. Maybe her generosity about paying Jacqueline's medical costs was more than to make sure it didn't go on her record with the insurance company. If she'd wired something wrong, it could ruin her reputation. Jane, you don't imagine it could be anything else but a careless mistake at the worst, do you? What could Thomasina have against Jacqueline?"

Jane said, "That's another thing we have to figure out. And you didn't ask her what she thought of Bitsy and Sandra, either, when you spoke to her, did you?"

"No. I didn't get a chance. She was already off and running about Joe Budley being the one who wanted the job badly enough to show up Sandra."

"We'll have to talk to Thomasina again." Jane made a mark by Thomasina's name like the one next to Carl Stringfield's name.

"Are we through with this chart yet?" Shelley asked impatiently. All the contents of the dishwasher had been neatly put away, and she sat back down across from Jane.

"For now. But now we need to get the events in order. Don't you dare sprawl over the table again. I promise you this is worthwhile, or will be."

"Wouldn't you rather be working on your book about Priscilla?" Shelley asked hopefully.

"I would. But suppose Bitsy caves in on the contract you drew up and we have to commit to doing the decorating before the police find out who's doing these things? We don't want to put ourselves in danger of becoming two more victims."

"Aren't we in more danger snooping into people's lives?"

Jane scoffed. "Shelley, people love talking about themselves to strangers. At least, most people do. Everybody has gripes they want to get off their chests. It helps them show off their admirable traits."

"Hmm," Shelley said. "Not everyone feels that way, though. Neither you nor I like sharing our personal lives with strangers. And how do we untangle those who are telling the truth from those who are lying through their teeth?"

"Instinct?" Jane suggested. "It's worked for us before."

"You're just trying to get me to forget this other chart you have in mind," Shelley said.

"No, I'm not. The other chart is pure fact. No speculation yet. Just a list of what's happened in chronological order before we start getting the timeline wrong." She flipped to the next page and wrote "shrimp."

"You already have it wrong," Shelley said with a laugh. "The shrimp episode was just the first thing we *knew* about. Jacqueline getting shocked happened before we even heard from Bitsy. And Thomasina's toolbox was stolen before we were involved as well. We only heard about it later."

"You're right," Jane said, amending her list. "So what was next?"

"Sandra's death, of course. Then the bomb scare with the toolbox, I think."

"Are we sure it wasn't Thomasina's toolbox coming back?"

"Yes, I forgot to mention that Mel told me so. Thomasina's was a big yellow plastic one. This one was steel."

"That didn't necessarily involve breaking in, then," Shelley said. "Someone could have easily taken it into work and put it in the basement. There's nothing much going on on the ground floor or in the kitchen yet."

"And then there was the wrecked Sheetrock soon after," Jane said.

"The return of the purse and the wrecked concrete on the sunporch were apparently the same night a few days later. Or was it the next day?" Shelley pondered. "I've already lost track of how long we've been on this job."

"Those two things had to be done by the same person, don't you imagine?" Jane asked. "Sneaking into the house with the purse. Probably through the coal chute. Then salting the concrete on the way out, or the other way around. I can't quite imagine two people discovering the coal chute and also being there the same night without running into each other."

"But the person who salted the concrete didn't necessarily know about the secret opening behind the bushes. All he or she had to do was go around the back at the other end of the house and dump the salt," Shelley commented. "And bringing back the purse makes no sense at all."

"Maybe it did," Jane replied. "It was the main thing the police were concentrating on when Sandra died. The mystery of what became of the purse she always wore strapped across her shoulder so firmly. Everybody noticed that."

"But why bring it back at all? What was the point of that?"

"I don't know. It's the weirdest part of the whole scenario. Maybe whoever took it was nervous about disposing of it, and thought it would take the heat off if the police got it back intact, with everything that was in it. For all the person knew, the police have some kind of arrangement with the city to hold and examine the trash that suspects put out."

"Pretty thin theory," Shelley complained.

"Got a better one?" Jane said.

"Not right now," Shelley admitted.

Jane thought a moment, then wrote down the fire in the Dumpster. "So what do all these have in common?"

"Nothing that I can see," Shelley said.

"Not one single thing, but maybe two things. The toolbox didn't really have a bomb in it. Nobody was in danger. It was a scare tactic. The destruction of the Sheetrock is the same. It made more work for Carl and

Evaline. It didn't harm anyone. The shrimp was the same. More work for Wesley, more cost for Bitsy. Except, of course, for Bitsy's lady friends who got sick from the smell."

"But the fire in the Dumpster was a real threat," Shelley said.

"Only to property, not people," Jane pointed out. "Nobody had any way of knowing you, Mel, and I would be in the house that night. Or anyone else, for that matter."

"So what does this chart tell us?" Shelley asked.

"That we need more coffee to get our minds working," Jane replied. "Let's look at this chart in different ways."

"What different ways?"

"Like how much physical strength the events we're considering took. How much expert knowledge? What sort of reach did they require? I'm wondering how high on the walls the Sheetrock damage was. I also wonder what the size of the coal chute is. Could the biggest person on the job climb through it?"

"Jane, it's time for you to go home and work on your book. You're trying to come to some conclusion with too little information. I think this might be the one time the police are much better equipped to figure this out. I'm sure Mel's experienced enough to question the same things and get the answers."

"Of course. But Mel's not the one considering signing a contract with Bitsy."

———

Jane took Shelley's advice and tried to work on her book, but she kept mentally fidgeting with her lists and charts. She created a file for them on her computer and started organizing the information, adding bits and pieces as she thought of them.

She was convinced she knew something she didn't know she knew. If she could dredge up more of what she'd seen, heard, and thought from the deepest part of her brain, she'd have an insight.

When she got into her disreputable station wagon to make yet another run to the grocery store, something she'd heard or observed on a previous trip kept tickling at the back of her mind.

She'd probably been concentrating on finding a parking space and dismissed whatever it was as irrelevant. She tried to think back to the week and remember where she'd been going when the thought struck her, but the harder she tried, the more elusive the memory became.

25

The next morning Shelley called Jane early. "Okay, I've thought about your list and what we need to know. We need to get over there and I'll tackle Thomasina, since I got along well with her earlier. You go after Carl, the Sheetrock guy."

"How am I supposed to strike up a personal conversation with him?" Jane asked. "The skills required of him are taking good measurements and having the strength to slap the Sheetrock on the walls. How much chitchat can I get out of that?"

"I don't know. But you can think of something. I've noticed a few times that he eats his lunch from home out on the verandah and is usually alone. You could take your own packed lunch and sit down next to him."

Jane didn't much like this idea, but since Shelley had endured her list making with fairly good grace, she felt obligated to give it a try. She got the kids off to school and packed herself a lunch. A ham sandwich, a couple of boiled eggs left over from the batch Shelley had made for her meal with Mel. A rather stale pack of Fritos, and a cold soda.

She put the soda and eggs in a plastic container filled with ice and stuffed it into a paper bag. When Shelley pulled out her garage and honked, Jane felt quite silly carrying a packed lunch. When she got into the minivan, she saw that Shelley had her own lunch in a big blue and white designer thermal bag.

"You packed that just to shame me."

"I packed it so you wouldn't be alone with Carl. Two people to question him are better than one. Besides, I left plenty of space for your lunch as well."

To their surprise, there was no law enforcement presence that morning. Everybody was hard at work, except Thomasina. She was loading her equipment into the back of a pristine white enclosed trailer attached to her truck. The back door was open, and Jane was fascinated as she peered in. It had a place for everything. Hooks for vast loops of different-size wires, bins for sockets of various configurations, drawers for screws and hooks for tools.

"Boy, would I like one of these," Jane exclaimed as they watched Thomasina putting everything away. "Just think how organized I could be."

Shelley looked at Jane and asked, "What do you have to haul around?"

"The very things you complain about. Dry cleaning, birdseed, loose receipts, the kids' book reports."

"Jane, that doesn't make sense," Shelley grouched. "Those aren't things you need to cart around. You buy them or pick them up, but you don't bring them into the house or garage and put them where they belong. It's not as if you're using them to do jobs away from home."

Jane ignored her and addressed Thomasina. "Why are you packing up? You haven't quit the job, have you?"

"No, but I've completed my work on the first side and nobody's ready for anything else yet. The other side of the upstairs isn't even cleared out, and Bitsy's not sure what appliances she needs in the kitchen and where they'll be placed." She paused and double-checked a notebook she pulled out of her back pocket against the content of the bins in the truck.

Nodding to herself, she went on. "I've got another couple of small jobs to do in the meantime. Wiring a screened porch for some people who want to enclose it for a garden room. Replacing a fuse box for another client who has been nagging me for a week." She slammed the back door of the trailer closed and locked it.

"Do you have to go this minute?" Shelley asked. "I have a couple of questions I want to ask you about Sandra."

"What kind of questions?" Thomasina asked suspiciously.

"What you thought of her," Shelley replied.

"That she didn't know what she was doing," Thomasina said bluntly. "She hired experts and wanted to meddle in things. Then there was all that feminist crap."

"You don't go along with that?" Jane asked.

"No, I don't. I'm a married woman with twin daughters. I don't want a contractor, male or female, wanting to keep touching me."

Jane and Shelley exchanged surprised glances, and Shelley asked, "Touching you?"

"Nothing really vulgar at first, just too chummy," Thomasina said, leaning against the trailer, which rocked slightly under her significant weight. "Wanting to lock arms when we walked around looking at where sockets would be placed. Pats on the shoulder for finishing a section of wall. Then one pat on the butt, which was when I told her off and to keep her hands to herself."

Jane was interested in Thomasina's verbal lashing of Sandra and wished she'd been present to hear it, but she was more taken by the concept of this supremely unattractive woman having a husband and children. "How old are your girls?" she asked.

Shelley gave Jane The Look.

Thomasina pulled a wallet from another pocket

and showed them a family picture. "This was taken a year ago when they were seven."

Her husband was a good four inches shorter than she and weighed at least fifty pounds less. He was fairly handsome. But it was the girls who were astonishing. Very pretty, but heavily made up.

"We had that picture taken to celebrate the day they won in their division," Thomasina said proudly. "Twins between five and ten years old. It's not a big category, but people think all twins are cute, just because they're twins. Of course they don't have to be identical, but the fraternal ones never even place. Don't know why their parents bother."

"Beauty pageants?" Shelley asked, concealing her distaste with amazing restraint.

"They love it. Little girls all like dressing up. And there's good money in it if they're attractive, spirited, and talented."

"What are their talents?" Jane asked.

"They dance," Thomasina said proudly. "My husband Walt and I taught them."

Jane's mental image of Thomasina and Walt dancing made her smile. "How nice. What kind of dancing do they do?"

"Tap and ballet both."

"How nice," Jane said. It was the only thing she could think to say, and she figured it was time to close the conversation before Shelley broke down and exposed her views of child beauty queens or asked if Thomasina was the ballet teacher, which would have sent Jane into hysterics.

Jane went on hurriedly, "We shouldn't be keeping you from getting on with your other jobs, though. Your time is obviously too valuable to waste on us."

Thomasina put away the wallet, checked her watch, and shook both their hands. "Hope you ladies are still around when I come back. I'll bring newer pictures of my girls to show you." With that, she hopped into the truck and roared off.

For a long moment both Jane and Shelley were silent.

"Who would have thought?" Shelley wondered.

"I just hope the Sheetrocker doesn't surprise us as much," Jane said.

They trapped Carl Stringfield having his lunch. It put theirs to shame. He had two warm pieces of bruschetta, a corned beef sandwich that looked as if the bread was baked from scratch, a salad with dried cranberries, and a piece of pumpkin pie.

He looked confused and slightly alarmed when Shelley sat down on one side of him and Jane on the other side.

"What a wonderful lunch you have," Shelley said. "Does your wife do this kind of thing every day?"

"What wife?"

"You fix all this yourself?"

"No, I have a neighbor taking a culinary class at the junior college and he makes it for me for practice. I have to write a report."

"So you're not married?" Shelley asked. "You must have a lot of free time for hobbies, I guess."

"I do a little fly fishing when I get the chance," he admitted.

A hard thing to comment on, Jane thought.

But Shelley took up the conversation. "Do you make your own flies?"

"Nope."

Shelley kept on. "Any other hobbies?"

He scratched his head. "Can't think of any."

"How do you like working with Evaline?"

"It's okay."

Shelley sighed, but continued the questioning. "Have you worked with her before?"

"Nope."

"I bet you'd like to, though. Her special paste must make the work go much faster."

"Hadn't given it any thought."

Jane had already finished her sandwich and munched her gummy Fritos before Shelley gave up.

"It surely has been interesting talking to you," she said with apparent sincerity. "I guess we should leave you to your lunch."

"Okay."

"Oh," Shelley said, "one more thing. What did you think of Sandra?"

"Not much," he said.

"Could you elaborate?"

"Not really."

26

When Shelley and Jane were on their way home, Shelley said, "That's the most aggressively boring person I've ever spoken to. No wonder he's not married. There would be no way to live with him unless you were in a coma."

"You're right. But maybe he just clams up around strangers. When someone comes to my door doing some nosy survey, I get very, very stupid and curt. Don't remember when I moved here. Don't remember my age."

"Why don't you just shut the door?" Shelley said.

"Because of my parents. When you're raised in the diplomatic corps, you learn to be overly polite."

"It didn't work on your sister."

"I know. But she was always cranky and difficult."

"Have you called her back yet?"

"Nope," Jane said, imitating Carl Stringfield.

"Okay," Shelley said.

"Wasn't the conversation with Thomasina interesting?" Jane said, changing the subject.

"Interesting, yes. But I can't see that it helps us figure out what's going on. I wish you hadn't veered off on those pathetic little girls."

"I had to before you *said* they were pathetic." Jane was laughing. "I couldn't help thinking of *Fantasia* when she said she and her husband taught the girls to dance. The pink elephants in tutus doing the ballet."

Shelley didn't think it was funny at all. "Can you imagine Sandra making a pass at her?"

"Hard to picture," Jane said. "But Thomasina nipped it in the bud, as you'd expect her to do. I'll bet she was more vulgar at the time than she let on to us."

"Maybe someone didn't tell Sandra off," Shelley said. "And that sort of unprofessional behavior on a job site might have truly upset another member of the crew."

"Have you anyone in mind?"

"Only Bitsy. I wonder if that's the real reason Bitsy fired her."

"You're not going to ask Bitsy that, are you?"

"I might."

"We've struck out on Thomasina. Her problem with Sandra was taken care of by telling her off and getting on with the job," Jane said. "And we got nothing from Carl. I still think our best suspects are Bitsy's ex-husband and Joe Budley."

"Both out of range for chatting up," Shelley said.

"Unfortunately," Jane agreed.

Shelley thought for a while and said, "Maybe I should talk to Paul about this."

"What does he know about renovations, feminism, or divorce?"

"Practically nothing. But he knows tons of people who know lots of other people. In fact, his attorney is a wealth of financial gossip. Paul never considers opening another restaurant without getting the whole history of the property he's considering and everybody who has owned or leased it. The attorney has an assistant who researches the history of any lawsuits or code violations."

"Would Paul be willing to find out about Neville Burnside and Joe Budley for us?"

"I'll ask. He doesn't like what he's heard about this renovation project anyway and may enjoy digging up some interesting dirt."

"Have you heard anything from Bitsy about this elusive contract we were supposed to have seen by now?"

"Not a peep. I called her early this morning to ask. She just fluttered around about how busy her lawyer was and how she couldn't catch up with him and thought he might be out of town on some kind of lecture tour to a law school."

"I don't believe that."

"Neither do I. But given the contract Sandra had drawn up and my new version, the lawyer has a lot to weed through," Shelley said.

"So what are you doing with the rest of your day, besides tackling your husband about Burnside and Budley?"

"Having a strongly worded talk with a caterer who's trying to charge me half again as much for the table service for a dinner Paul's giving for his employees. The caterer we've used for the last two years went out of business when an employee passed along hepatitis. Contagious diseases can kill a successful catering business. This new one is giving me an outrageous bid and the event is in two weeks. I don't have time to interview others. I'll just have to beat this one into submission."

"Shelley, sometimes you amaze me with the specialized information you have at your fingertips. I know absolutely nothing about catering and you seem to know everything about it. This is fascinating."

"Not really. It's simply that Paul insists on these dinners three or four times a year and I agree it's good for his business. A nice perk. And we couldn't possibly serve them the Greek fast food they're up their elbows in every day. He used to have an employee plan the dinners until I butted in and comparison-shopped and realized she was taking us to the cleaners and getting big kickbacks. That's how I got stuck with the job."

"But there's nothing you enjoy more than butting heads with people trying to rip you off, and you know it," Jane said.

Shelley grinned. "It's one of my best skills. So are you working on your book today, since we're not getting anywhere with Bitsy and her elusive attorney?"

"Yes. I've thought of a new twist for the plot I'm really excited about. Want to hear about it?"

"No. I'll wait until the book is in the stores. You don't want to drain away a good idea recounting it to someone else."

Jane had awakened in a rage the previous night when the cats decided to sharpen their claws on her bedspread. Before drifting off to sleep, she'd realized why she'd dawdled on getting the novel finished. Priscilla had gone soft and comfy. She'd gotten boring. Her life was going too well.

The essence of fiction, Jane thought, was conflict, the more the better.

So how about if a previously unknown older, illegitimate half-brother showed up with documentation claiming to prove Priscilla's beloved home was really his?

She loved the idea. Priscilla would have something dear to her to fight for. Priscilla loved her house on the cliff overlooking a surly sea more than she'd ever loved anything else.

Supposing the documents were true but the person presenting them wasn't who he said he was? A real illegitimate brother had once existed and this man had seized his papers.

Maybe it was a bit trite, but Jane was fired up. What would Priscilla do? Would she find out the man was a fraud? If so, would she feel compelled to find her real half-brother? Not if she had any sense. Maybe she could find out about him without his knowing.

Priscilla could hire someone to hunt him down. An honorable and necessarily devilishly good-looking man she imagines for a while she might have fallen in love with but later finds out that he's in on the fraud. Or maybe not. Maybe he's already married. Maybe he's not married, but has a terminal disease and . . . Or maybe Priscilla's doctor has mistakenly told her she's the one with the terminal condition?

So many intriguing avenues of busy plot to whip into shape.

And a lot more fun than trying to pry the truth out of the workers at the renovation. In her novel, she herself was in control. She'd know the truth, even if Priscilla didn't.

But who could guess which, in real life, if any of the workers or their ex-relatives was responsible for the vandalism and very probably Sandra's death?

27

It was four days before Shelley came over to Jane's house at lunchtime to tell her what Paul had found out. Jane had practically forgotten what Shelley was talking about. She'd been completely immersed in her novel all weekend and Monday, and hadn't even taken the time to shower or comb her hair on Tuesday morning.

"Here's the deal," Shelley said. "There may be more, but I wanted to share what Paul's attorney's assistant has already dragged up. Budley is first. He's had lots of lawsuits and small-claims-court records. But most of them, the assistant says, are just nutcases trying to get out of paying him."

"Oh?" Jane said, once she'd recognized what Shelley was all het up about.

"I don't smell coffee," Shelley said. "You're going to need it to pay attention."

Jane started a big pot of coffee, and Shelley graciously waited until Jane had knocked back half a cup.

"As an example"—Shelley took up her story—"Budley was doing a big job putting in a basement media room and had it almost it done. There was a horrific storm that sent water gushing through where the basement windows had been sealed. He had to redo the base woodwork and carpets and didn't meet his deadline. Are you listening, Jane?"

"I am."

"Budley invoked the Acts of God clause and got his money. Apparently he'd had the sealed windows inspected by the city code guy who approved Budley's work."

"Did the city code guy get in trouble in turn?"

"Nope, the clients tried to go after him but failed to get a judgment. The code guy had made extensive notes of his visit. He'd told the people they had to fill in around the foundation where water collected to get approval. They didn't do it.

"Another lawsuit the assistant cited was when some artsy-fartsy client had six old French doors he'd picked up at a garage sale that he wanted installed so his guests and family could look out over the patio and garden. As soon as it turned cold, the doors shrank and the glass in them shattered. Budley had apparently learned a lesson on keeping paperwork from the media room fiasco and was able to produce copies of letters that he'd by sent registered mail, telling the man the doors weren't the right size and wouldn't survive a cold Chicago winter. The man hadn't agreed to shave them down to size because he said they'd be out of proportion. Budley kept that letter from the client as well."

"Clearly not his fault."

"Right. I remember the time Paul had two inches of mirror put in around the ceiling of our study to reflect the lights. When it got cold, the molding and walls shrank and the mirrors all cracked."

"You never told me about that. I guess you replaced them? I've always admired the way the light bounces around in the study."

"Now you know how to do that. Leave a bit of room."

Shelley returned to the subject she'd started first. "The assistant still had other suits to examine and we'll see what turns up. My own opinion, for what it's worth, is that Budley's probably competent but is so offensive and tactless that he annoys people into finding fault with his work."

"You'd feel that way, too. I've never seen you as mad as when he called us 'girls.' I was afraid you were having a stroke."

"No, I save strokes for dealing with the IRS," Shelley said with a laugh.

"Anything on Neville Burnside yet?"

"Do you have any more of those icky granola bars?"

"I bought two more boxes of them. Don't pretend you don't like them."

Shelley munched down two of them while Jane, who was sick of them, made two ham sandwiches.

Shelley looked at her watch. "It is way past time for lunch. Thanks. Anyway, the attorney's assistant hasn't even gotten to him yet," she said while slathering mustard on the sandwich. "She's still following up on Joe Budley."

"Is this costing Paul wads of money?"

Shelley laughed. "Considering the size of the annual retainer Paul pays this attorney and the fact that he admitted he didn't have anything for his legal assistant to do this week, he's glad to do it gratis. Or so he says. He told Paul all the material will go in a file and someday when someone else asks about Budley, he'll just dig out the file and impress the hell out of them with his quick work."

"Good thinking."

"Paul is often stunned by the speed of his research into property. Now we know how he does it. He keeps files on everybody he's ever checked out. Are you going to tell Mel we're doing this?"

"Hmm. I hadn't thought of that. I think it would be best if we waited until we have all the information."

"That's a good idea. Paul's attorney might already have a file on Neville Burnside and will knock our socks off again with his promptness."

"The one time we met him, I thought he was a very

nasty man. Most of the people I know who are divorced, no matter what kind of settlement is imposed on them, get over it and go on with their lives."

"Maybe it's too soon for him. I think he's so angry that he could have done all the vandalizing. But not in person. He'd be too obvious if anyone saw him lurking around. Maybe he hired one of Bitsy's discontented workers to do the sabotage."

"That's an interesting theory," Jane said. "But it would have cost him too much. I do think it's likely that others have inquired about him or brought suits against him. This attorney Paul uses sounds like more of a detective than a lawyer."

"That's why Paul pays the big bucks. The guy loves to get the dirt on people. I guess it's an instinct."

"One we also share," Jane said.

"Bite your tongue," Shelley said with laugh. "Oh, I forgot to tell you something else. I finally met the plumber."

"I'd forgotten there has to be a plumber. Why haven't we come across him yet?"

"It's a she, Jane," Shelley said. "Introduced herself as Hank. I can't imagine what that's short for. For some reason she wasn't on the list of workers and phone numbers Bitsy gave me."

"She must have been one of the earliest to work once the walls were down in that section. Doesn't plumbing have to come first?"

"I have no idea. But if you think back, the first time

we looked at the renovated part there were pipes stubbed out in the bathrooms and in the kitchen."

"Count on you to notice that. I didn't. So did you talk to Hank?"

"To my sorrow, I did. She said right out that Sandy Anderson was a cross between Eleanor Roosevelt and Mother Teresa."

"What an odd combination," Jane said. "I don't get the connection."

Shelley said, "I think I do. How much do you know about Eleanor Roosevelt?"

"Not as much as I'd like. Why?"

"Some recent scholars have suggested that after Eleanor found out about Lucy Mercer having an affair with Franklin, Eleanor and her longtime women friends became, let us say, much closer friends."

"You mean lesbians? Oh, now I get it."

"Hank went on haranguing about their feminist group and how it would never have gotten off the ground if it hadn't been for wonderful Sandy. She was both a hard and a tenderhearted person. Always so supportive of everyone in the group. She called Sandra a good example of 'tough love' and actually got a bit teary about her dying."

"No! I can't imagine that," Jane exclaimed.

"But she recovered quickly. She demanded that I go back to the Merchandise Mart and present my recommendations on the swirly hot tub thing that they're putting in the master bath. Told me in no uncertain terms to be sure to consider only the ones that are left-handed."

"Left-handed? What does that mean?"

"I think it means they hook into the plumbing at the end she's stubbed out, instead of having to be installed with the back of it the wrong way around."

"What did you tell her?"

"That we weren't yet under contract and were still waiting for a better one. She went ballistic. How dare I argue about the contract? Sandra, or Sandy, as she insisted on calling her, could never be wrong about anything. She thought it was a wonderful contract."

"Did you tell her . . . ?"

"You bet I did. I told her that everyone else on the job that I'd talked to had slashed through theirs and gotten it changed. That really knocked her for a loop. Later I saw her go out to her truck. When I was leaving, Hank was sitting there behind the steering wheel, flipping pages of what looked like her contract."

"If she's telling the truth, she's certainly not a suspect in Sandra's death."

"Jane, we don't really know if *anybody* has told us the truth."

"I guess that's true. But Henrietta and Jacqueline were quite frank with us. And so were Evaline and Thomasina. Even Bitsy's inclined to spill her guts at every opportunity."

"I hate to admit this," Shelley said, "but I'm starting to feel sorry for Bitsy. I know Sandra was her own-free-will choice of contractor, but so many things have gone wrong on the project. Bitsy has to be thinking it's her fault."

Shelley opened the foil on a third granola bar. "Maybe so. But she's still plowing along with it."

"If I were she, God forbid, I'd have taken my loss by now and turned it back over to the township to tear down."

"I'm so glad to hear you say that," Jane said.

"I know. You should just back out."

"I can't do that to you."

"Sure you can. You're so excited suddenly about your book. That's what you're meant to be putting your brains to work on. I can do the decorating myself. Or find someone else who has the skills and interest. But only if Bitsy antes up what I think is fair."

Jane knew Shelley wholeheartedly believed what she was saying. But the book had already taken her years and she would hate to disappoint her best friend.

28

Wednesday morning Jane got a call from Evaline.

"Carl and I will be finishing up our work by noon, if not earlier. And I have some good news to tell you and Shelley. I'd like to celebrate. Could you two come to dinner at my apartment?"

"I'll have to check with Shelley. But it sounds like a good idea to me. Can you give me a hint about your good news?"

Evaline laughed. "No. I have to save it for tonight. Would seven be too late?"

"That's fine. I can feed my kids at six. I'll get back to you."

Jane caught Shelley just as she was leaving for another fight with the caterer.

"I'll either have it sorted out or will be interviewing someone else I've heard about long before then. I can make it. Did she tell you what the good news is?"

"She's saving it for dinner."

"I have got to run. I'll pick you up at quarter to seven."

Jane spent another day at the computer with Priscilla and wished she hadn't committed to the dinner. She'd rather have continued her work while she was on a roll. But she'd promised Evaline they'd be there.

"How'd the meeting with the caterer go?" Jane asked as she got into Shelley's minivan.

"I won. I never really doubted that I would. Where are we going?"

Jane gave her Evaline's address, and they arrived just on time.

The apartment was on the first floor. Evaline greeted them at the door before they even knocked. "I saw you pull up. I'm running the tiniest bit late. I forgot to start the beans on time. Come in."

Her apartment was tiny but well-kept. It must have come already furnished, Jane guessed. The pictures on the walls of the living room seemed somewhat generic, not a reflection of what little they knew of Evaline. The furniture was cheap but clean and comfortable. Evaline, dressed in a short khaki skirt and a flowered shirt, asked them what they wanted to drink. "I have iced tea, sodas, or beer. And I even bought Shelley some bottled water and a six-pack of RC Cola for you, Jane."

She was back in a moment with their drinks. She sat down beside Shelley on the sofa. "I heard from the patent attorney yesterday. He has a guy in the patent office he's worked with for a long time," she said. "He called him and asked if he could hurry it through and the guy said he would."

"That's wonderful," Jane said. "I'm so glad for you."

"It gets even better," she said with a grin. "The patent attorney has talked to some joint-venture investors and they're considering funding me."

Jane was delighted and put down her drink to give Evaline a congratulatory handshake. But she spilled a bit of it on her hand. "Oops, I'll have to wash my hand first."

On entering the kitchen Jane noticed a pot on the stove that was almost bubbling over and turned the burner off. Then she washed her hands and looked around for a paper towel to dry them. Not seeing any, she opened a drawer to find a dishcloth. The first drawer was full of silverware. The next drawer down held the dishcloths. As she lifted one out, she saw something under it. A little brown leather notebook with a name stamped on it in gold. She picked it up with a fresh dishcloth.

In the living room, Shelley was asking Evaline when she thought she'd get the patent. Evaline started to reply, but sniffed and said, "Oh, dear. I think the gravy's burning. I forgot to turn off the stove." She hurried to the kitchen and came to a sudden stop when she saw Jane.

"What are you doing with that?"

"Oh, Evaline, I'm so sorry. I was just looking for something to dry my hands and found this."

"You're not going to tell anyone, are you?"

"I have to," Jane said.

Evaline reached for the pot where the gravy was still boiling-hot. "No, you won't," she said. She grabbed the handle of the pot and made a swinging motion with it, but it slipped out of her hand and hit the floor. Hot, thick brown gravy splashed back on her bare legs, and she screamed.

As Shelley ran into the room, Jane put down the little book and scrambled to the sink with a handful of more dishcloths to get them wet. "Call 911, Shelley. She's burned herself badly."

Shelley already had her cell phone in her hand, and while she waited for an answer said, "Jane, dab. Don't wipe."

Evaline had collapsed on the floor, still screaming.

After the emergency medical technicians had taken Evaline away, Shelley asked, "What happened?"

"She was trying to throw the boiling-hot gravy at me, and it came back on her. I'll explain in a minute, but first call Mel and tell him to call the nearest hospital and order them not to release her. She killed Sandra. The evidence is on the kitchen counter."

Shelley dialed the police station as Jane started cleaning up the gravy from the floor.

"I need to talk to Mel VanDyne immediately,"

Shelley was saying. "You can't contact him? Why? Never mind. Call the hospitals and find out which one the emergency people took Evaline Berman from this address," she said, reeling off the street address and apartment number. "She's the one who murdered the woman on the case Detective VanDyne is on. Tell them not to release her."

She hung up and said, "Jane, stop cleaning. Let's get out of here."

They were both so shaken that they just sat in Shelley's minivan for a few minutes, trying to calm down enough for Shelley to drive. In a shaking voice, Jane explained about looking for a dishcloth and finding Sandra's little brown notebook in the drawer.

"How did you know it was hers?"

"It had her name stamped on the front. Did you leave the door to the apartment unlocked?"

"Yes," Shelley said as she fumbled to get the ignition key in and start the car.

For once in her life, she drove slowly and carefully.

Jane had gravy all over her knees from kneeling and trying to get the gravy off Evaline, and went straight to the basement to take her slacks off. Shelley followed her. "There should be clean jeans in the dryer. Keep very quiet. I don't want Kate and Todd to know about this."

"You're still shaking, and you're as white as a ghost. Do you want to come to my house?"

"You're as pale as I am. Let's go sit out on the patio.

I'll take the portable phone with me, so if Mel calls back, I can grab the call before one of the kids picks it up."

They sat outside for quite a long time, speaking in low tones. "At least I had the common sense not to get my own fingerprints on the notebook."

"Good for you. Katie's not on the phone line, is she?" Shelley said.

"No. A little red light would come on the portable if she were."

It was dark, and the evening was turning chilly. Jane went inside and peeked in each child's room. Katie was listening to loud music while supposedly doing her homework. Jane pulled herself together well enough to say, "Katie, don't use the phone for a while. I'm expecting a call." Katie nodded.

Todd had his computer on and was mumbling to himself and punching numbers into the little adding machine. Jane told him he'd better stop working on the prime numbers in a few minutes and do his homework.

"Already did it."

"Mrs. Nowack and I are going to sit outside for a while. If you need anything, you can find me."

She got out a couple of sweaters and on the way through the kitchen, poured two glasses of wine. "This will warm us up a bit," she said, handing Shelley one of the glasses and a sweater.

"I'm so sorry it was Evaline," Shelley said. "I know

you liked her. Do you think she was responsible for all the other things that happened at the House of Seven Mabels?"

Jane shrugged. "I don't know. I'm sort of sick even thinking about it."

"Did you open the notebook?"

"No. I was holding it with a dishcloth and looking for a place to put it somewhere she wouldn't find it and dispose of it before we could contact Mel. But she caught me holding it. I did like her until she tried to disfigure me with the hot gravy."

"How did she think that would save *her*?"

"I doubt she was thinking at all. She was lashing out at someone who'd suddenly become a threat. That's all."

The phone rang. Jane pushed the button and said, "Mel?"

"Are you okay?"

"Shaken, but not stirred," Jane said.

"I'm swamped and can't talk now, but I wanted to be sure you were home and safe," Mel said. "Go to bed. I'll call you in the morning."

"You do have Evaline locked up somewhere, don't you?"

"We sure do."

"That's all I need to know."

29

Mel called Jane at 8:30 the next morning.

"Where were you when I needed to get in touch with you?" Jane asked.

"On a stakeout at what Shelley calls the House of Seven Gables."

"Seven Mabels. Why?"

"I was thinking there hadn't been anything bad happening there for a couple of days and it was time for another event. So I got four officers to hide in and around the place."

"Did something happen?"

"Yep! It did. We caught a kid about nineteen pry-ing loose one of the pieces of plywood over the windows to get inside. He'd been equipped with a gallon of gasoline and a bag of dry rags."

"Good Lord! Who was he? What did he say?"

"First he wet his pants. Then he told us his dad used to do a lot of jobs for Neville Burnside. When his dad died a of couple weeks ago, Burnside contacted him."

"So this kid with the wet crotch was responsible for all the vandalism?"

"No. Just a lot of it. Evaline admits she rigged the electrical and did the shrimp deal to discredit Sandra. And the fake bomb toolbox and returning the purse. Everything else she vehemently denies."

"What about Evaline's burns?"

"She's in bad shape and will be under treatment for them for quite a while. But in a prison hospital, not the one she first went to."

"Did she confess that she killed Sandra?"

"Yes, but she claims it was accidental."

"Accidental? How?"

"I'll explain later. In fact, that's why I'm calling you. It'll be in the evening papers and I want to meet with everyone involved in the renovation at the house to give them the information before they read about it. Eleven o'clock this morning at the house. Can you and Shelley be there?"

"Of course we will."

"Janey, are you all right?"

"A lot better knowing Evaline's not free to come after me again."

"I'm sending an officer over in a few minutes to interview you and Shelley about last night. Are you up to it? I don't think I should be the one to do it."

She and Shelley made their statements. The officer, a young man who looked too young to have even finished high school, much less college and police training, recorded what they said and told them he'd have it typed up and they'd get to read and correct anything before they signed it in a day or maybe two.

When they arrived at the House of Seven Mabels, another problem had cropped up. A truck was parked in the driveway with big fancy windows lashed firmly to it. Jane and Shelley were allowed into the house by a uniformed police officer and told Detective VanDyne was waiting for them upstairs.

They could hear Bitsy long before they got halfway up the stairs. She was yelling at someone. "I didn't authorize this. I'm the owner and I don't know what you're doing here."

They walked into the room as one of two men they'd never seen before handed her an invoice. "Your contractor, Sandra Anderson, signed this. She said the windows had dry rot and placed a special order."

Bitsy snatched the paper away from them and crumpled it. "My damned contractor is dead! And there's nothing wrong with the windows that I know about. This is just too much."

Mel was standing in a corner of the room by the door. Jane and Shelley went to stand beside him.

Bitsy raved on as Carl Stringfield came into the room.

Mel said, "Mrs. Burnside, I'm afraid you're going to have to sort this out later with these gentlemen. Everybody's here and I have to tell all of you some things."

Carl looked around and said, "Evaline isn't here yet."

"That what we're talking about," Mel said. "Let's go to the dining room where there are chairs," he said, leading the way downstairs.

When they were all seated, he said, "Evaline Berman was arrested last night for the murder of Sandra Anderson. She's currently hospitalized for burns to her legs."

There was a collective gasp from everyone but Jane, Shelley, Mel, and the officer standing at the doorway.

"Several officers and I staked out this house last night," Mel went on, "and caught a young man prying the plywood off from one of the windows. He was equipped with materials to burn the house down."

"No!" Bitsy screamed, starting to leap from her chair.

Mel, sitting next to her, took her arm. "Mrs. Burnside, sit down, please. He claimed he'd been hired to do it by your ex-husband, who's currently under arrest and being questioned. We have accountants going through all his bank records."

Bitsy subsided, smiling radiantly.

"As for Evaline Berman, she attempted to attack Mrs. Jeffry in her apartment at the same time the young man was being taken away."

"Attacked her?" Carl asked, shaking his head with disbelief.

"With a pot full of boiling gravy," Mel said.

A silence fell. Mel let it stretch out for a moment, then explained, "She'd invited Jane Jeffry and Shelley Nowack to dinner to brag about her patent. Jane went to the kitchen to wash something sticky off her hand and found Sandra Anderson's notebook in a drawer. Evaline came in and saw Jane holding it, and tried to throw boiling gravy at Jane, but accidentally dumped it on herself.

"Evaline later claimed that Sandra was trying to steal the secret ingredient in her patent. Sandra's notebook might bear that out. It contained a note about a food ingredient, and the name, address, and telephone number of her patent attorney. He's been questioned and claims she did contact him.

"I'm afraid that's all I'm at liberty to say at this time."

As he was finishing, there was a knock at the door of the dining room. The officer standing behind Mel opened it to the men with the truck full of windows.

"May we speak to Mrs. Burnside now?"

"No," Bitsy said. "Shelley, I have your contract ready."

"Keep it," Shelley said. "Jane and I have decided we don't want the job."

Bitsy's smile faded. "My best friends have turned into traitors?"

"We're hardly your best friends, Bitsy," Shelley said.

Bitsy looked around the table at the others. "Are the rest of you bailing out on me, too?"

Carl just looked down at his hands.

Henrietta went first. "Jacqueline and I are."

Wesley said, "It's up to Mrs. Stanley to decide for herself, but I won't be back."

"Me neither." Thomasina spoke up.

"I can't afford to be involved in something like this," Joe Budley said, standing up to leave.

Mel motioned at Budley to stay.

Hank was getting teary. She looked daggers at Bitsy and said, "You're responsible for Sandy's death as much as what's-her-name with the gravy. I wouldn't work for you if you gave me a million dollars!"

Bitsy said in a dead, calm voice, "That's it."

She rummaged through her purse and pulled out a cell phone. Punching a few numbers, she said, "Jennifer? Is that you? Listen. Book me a flight to Bermuda for the day after tomorrow. First class. Hurricane? I don't care if there's a hurricane! Okay, okay, Carmel then. Best hotel. The biggest suite they have. And have champagne waiting."

She hung up and punched in another number. "Put me through to Brian. Right *now*." While she waited, she ran her hand through her hair, which stood up like a bad wig.

"Brian, Bitsy Burnside here. Stop whatever you're doing and draw up a quitclaim deed on the house, signing it back over to the township. And call the accountant and tell him to figure out all the workers' wages as of today. I'll be over to sign the checks and the deed in an hour. And prepare a lawsuit against my husband and his company for destruction of property."

She flung the cell phone back into her purse and looked at Mel.

"May I go now? I'm entitled to a fabulous nervous breakdown in luxury."

Jane and Shelley went home, enormously relieved. "I'm glad you turned the contract down without even asking me," Jane said.

"I realized it was hopeless and you really didn't want to do it. And I didn't, either. No matter what the contract said about money. But there's one thing I'd still like to know."

"The secret ingredient."

"Right."

When Mel came back later, they appealed to him. "We promise, cross our hearts and hope to die, never to reveal the secret ingredient. But please, please tell us," Jane said.

"Since the site is bookmarked on Evaline's computer, I can. But I hold you to the promise. She was researching the Great Wall of China. There was a lot of material about the way the stones were finished and fired. But the kicker was a remark about the mortar and how it had held together so well over so many centuries. Seems that bits of it had been analyzed and one of the ingredients was rice flour. Sandra had written that down in her notebook."

Shelley harked back to Evaline claiming it was an accident. "But couldn't it have been an argument, leading to a brawl, that resulted in Sandra simply falling down the stairs?" she asked Mel.

"Not after what she tried to do to Jane. You're going to have to testify, Jane, if it comes to a trial. Evaline is a loose cannon when she's crossed."

Jane hadn't been listening carefully. She nearly slapped her head. "I remember what I couldn't remember! I wasn't driving *myself*. That's where I was going wrong. Evaline was driving."

Shelley said, "What on earth are you talking about?"

"Something has been niggling at the back of mind for days. When I went with Evaline to see her patent attorney, she asked if we could stop off at the grocery store to pick something up. She came back with a heavy bag all sealed up."

"Jane, get to the point," Shelley said.

"I am. As we left the parking lot, I thought I saw Sandra's car coming in. Evaline said the car was the wrong shade of blue, and I believed her. But I was right. It *was* Sandra's car. And I also believe that Evaline knew, too. But she didn't want to let on. That's why she went on about how many cars look alike. Just to get me off the subject.

"I'll bet Sandra was following us, lurking in the parking lot and rushing into the store to consult with the checkout people about what Evaline had just bought. That must have been how she knew it was rice flour."

"We shouldn't be surprised," Shelley said with a laugh. "Remember when the kids were babies and got upset stomachs and we had to give them rice flour pablum? If it's so good at stopping up babies, it's sure to be what held up the Great Wall of China."

"Too bad we didn't know what the ingredient was earlier," Jane said with a laugh. Turning to Mel, she said, "Just one more domestic detail mothers know and single men don't."